MURDER IN THE RABID DOG

A 1951 Philip Bryce mystery

Peter Zander-Howell

Copyright © 2024 Peter Zander-Howell

All rights reserved.

Certain well-known historical persons are mentioned in this work. All other characters and events portrayed in this book are fictitious, and any similarity to real persons, alive or dead, is coincidental and not intended by the author. Real-world locations in this book may have been slightly altered.

No part of this book may be reproduced, or stored in a retrieval system, or transmitted in any form or by any means, electronic, mechanical, photocopying, recording, or otherwise, without the express permission of the publisher.

ISBN - 9798345392089

INTRODUCTION

Philip Bryce is an unusual policeman. A Cambridge-educated barrister, he joined the Metropolitan Police in 1937 under Lord Trenchard's accelerated promotion scheme.

After distinguished army service in WW2, by 1949 he was Scotland Yard's youngest Detective Chief Inspector.

A series of highly successful cases led to a double-jump promotion. Now a Detective Chief Superintendent, he leads a small team dealing with those serious cases where the Yard's help has been requested – either from within the Metropolitan Police area or elsewhere in the country.

Bryce married in 1949, and at the time of this book he and his wife have a new baby daughter, Fleur.

Bryce is something of a polymath, and has a number of outside interests – railways and cricket near the top of the list.

CHAPTER 1

Saturday, 20th October, 1945

The Rabid Dog alehouse had occupied a site in the heart of London's docklands for a good hundred and fifty years. It was not, many would agree, an appealing name for a pub, although that by no means deterred the drinkers who chose it for their watering hole. The origin of the unusual name might have been lost to history, had not a regular repeated a tale told by his grandfather (who said he had heard from his own grandfather) that the tavern was far more conventionally called *The Dog* at one time.

Allegedly, the 'Rabid' had been colloquially introduced in the 1820s, following a spate of adulteration to the ales sold. Such sharp and sometimes dangerous practice was widespread at the time, before regulation and legal penalties held producers and vendors accountable for standards of edibility and potability. There were various different substances added. One in particular, 'hard multum', was in widespread use in lower class establishments, and the subject of critical comment from Charles Dickens, amongst others.

It was the wives of those Georgian patrons of The Dog who were said to have complained to one another about a more vicious turn in the behaviour of their menfolk after drinking at the tavern. A proliferation of split lips and black eyes gave rise to the name change amongst the women, which was later more formally recorded when the pub's battered and illegible old signboard was replaced.

Very little had changed at the pub in the intervening years. It was still only licensed to sell ales. And it was still the case that this was no great disadvantage to most of its clientele, given that few could ever afford a tot of spirits and were in any case happy to take a slower, cheaper route, to inebriation.

As might be expected in an establishment serving lower-cost beers, the profits of the house were not great, and no landlord had sufficient funds – or inclination to spend what funds he did have – to refurbish the premises. Nevertheless, the solid oak benches, tables, and bar had withstood a hundred and fifty years of use very well, their highly polished patina achieved by the actions of spills, tobacco stains and constant use, rather than any vigorous housekeeping on the part of successive publicans.

In the way of similar houses in the less salubrious parts of cities, the Rabid Dog had seen more than a few brawls and beatings. Barely a month after the end of WW2, the pub was also the scene of a murder.

On a typically crowded Saturday night, a man was standing in the smoke-filled fug at the single bar, trying to get the attention of the overworked barmaid. Spotting his signal, she made one of her own to indicate that she had seen him and would serve him when she could.

A woman entered the pub alone at this point. First pausing in the doorway to take her bearings, she pushed her way through the noisy throng until she was standing behind the man. Seconds later, she turned and pushed her way out again. As she did so, the man seemed to fold up, and despite being partially propped up by the bar and those standing around him, he slid to the floor.

Initially, it was assumed that he had drunk too much – not an unusual occurrence in that, or any other, pub. But as the barmaid knew, the man hadn't as yet actually imbibed anything. At least, not on those premises.

When the landlord, intending to move the man into the street, managed to persuade the surrounding customers to clear a sufficient path, blood on the floor quickly changed the picture and alerted him to the gravity of the situation.

With some delay (the pub had no telephone), an ambulance was summoned. The crew immediately pronounced the man dead, and seconds later announced that he had a wound in his back.

The landlord, wishing that he had been quick enough to drag the body outside so that he could pretend the death had not occurred in his tavern, gloomily awaited a visit from the police. A number of his customers who, for reasons of their own preferred to avoid all contact with the police, quickly emptied their jars and left.

In due course, PC Paine arrived, followed shortly after by DS Blakely and a police surgeon. The latter, who was speaking to the policemen but audible to those nearby, announced that the man had been shot. Paine was despatched to a police box to request the attendance of a more senior officer.

In the meantime, Sergeant Blakely followed procedure and talked to those who admitted being closest to the dead man as he stood at the bar.

It took half an hour for the Divisional Detective Inspector, Stanley Gilbert, to arrive. Blakely quickly briefed his boss and pointed to five customers who had been segregated on one side of the room. The landlord had rejoined the barmaid and his wife behind the bar, coincidentally all standing in the positions they had been in when the shooting occurred.

It was now almost closing time. The DDI ordered his subordinates to take the names and addresses of the remaining drinkers before driving them out. He guessed that some bystanders, who may well have been helpful to his enquiries, had already made themselves scarce.

Of the five men whom the Sergeant had said were nearest to the deceased when he met his end, Gilbert asked, "What happened, then?"

The DDI heard five almost identical stories. The victim was standing immediately behind those who were leaning on the bar. He, and all the men around him, were facing the bar. One said he became aware of a woman pushing up behind the victim. She stood behind him for only a second or two, then turned and went out.

As she left, three of the witnesses noted that she had long blonde hair and was carrying what looked like a large shopping bag. Nobody claimed to have seen her face. One man said she was looking down as she hurried out, hair covering the sides of her face. Nobody was prepared to estimate her age either, although all agreed that she "... didn't move like an old 'un..." and was "...prob'ly on the younger side..."

"Take names and addresses, Sergeant," ordered the DDI, and turned to question the bar staff instead. "What do you know about the dead man?"

The three shrugged their shoulders in unison.

"Nothing," said the barmaid, shaking out a noisesome-looking tea towel and drying pint pots as she spoke. She was of an age and size for whom the description 'barmaid' was a misnomer and somehow most unflattering. Barmatron would have been more fitting for her in every respect.

She continued. "He's not an old reg'lar in the way our other customers are. First spotted him about a month ago. He's been in and out three or four times a week since then. Buys a drink and sits down if he can; just stands where you are if he can't."

She breathed over a smear on a glass before buffing it. "Doesn't speak to me – difficult with all the din in 'ere – just points to the mild tap. I hold up a pint glass and he nods. Bit of a loner; never seen 'im talk to anyone else, neither." She looked across at the landlord and his wife. Both agreed that this was also their understanding.

Shoving the tea towel into the new jar she was drying, the barmaid scratched her head with her free hand, her fingers disappearing into a poorly pinned and unstable nest of dyed black hair, loosening it further. "Not a boozer, though. Don't think he's ever had more than the one pint on a visit. Always has the right money."

Gilbert tried the usual re-phrasing of his questions, attempting to tease out additional information by every means. As with his five earlier witnesses, he soon realised there was no meat to pick off the bones of what he was hearing and changed tack. "What about this woman, then? Tell me about her."

Neither the barmaid nor the landlord had noticed her at all, but the landlord's wife said she had seen the back of her as she went out.

"Lots of blonde 'air. Eye-catchin', like them others told you. I'd've remembered that 'air if I'd seen it afore. I reckon she'd never been in."

All the witnesses denied hearing a gunshot but said – and the DDI could well believe it – that there was a great deal of noise in the bar, including a wireless playing at the time, and people had to shout to make themselves heard. Even so, he thought it was almost certain that the gun had been fitted with a silencer.

By the time the detectives left the pub, they had few clues to work with: an unknown blonde-haired woman, carrying a shopping bag, had stood by the murdered man moments before he fell.

Other avenues of investigation were quickly explored in turn. The most solid evidence in the first forty-eight hours after the shooting came from the *post mortem* and the ballistics report. Two shots had been fired from a 0·32 calibre pistol. The gun was never found.

The most promising line of enquiry at this time was soon snuffed out. The slain man had carried an identification card in the name of Leonard Bowen. It turned out to be a forgery.

Over the next week, very little of help to the investigation emerged. The only discovery of note was a canvas shopping bag with a hole surrounded by burn marks. This was found in a nearby street and was quickly established to be a commonly available article. It yielded no clues.

The investigation slowed down.

Without sufficient manpower to mount rapid and wide-ranging house to house enquiries, more than two weeks passed before a member of the investigating team found a man who let out rooms.

Eric Mannington told DS Blakely that he carried out a fortnightly change of bedsheets for all his occupants. This agreed arrangement required him to strip off the bottom sheet and replace it with the top sheet, the bed then being made up with a fresh top sheet beneath the blankets. He would also mop the linoleum in each room at the same time. These practices, quite common in such houses, legally enabled him to use his duplicate keys to enter each of the rooms and keep an eye on things, in much the same way that chamber maids did (albeit more frequently and with additional services) in hotels.

Under threat of arrest for obstruction and withholding information, Mannington very reluctantly admitted one of his tenants might have disappeared, leaving behind his meagre possessions. It emerged that the lodger had taken the room only a few weeks before, paying three months' rent in advance, plus a generous gratuity for the accommodating landlord. Terms had been agreed on a strictly 'no ID and no name given' basis, with the promise that all future rent – plus repeat bonuses – would be paid in the same way.

Shown a mortuary picture of the deceased, Mannington confirmed it was his lodger and agreed that he had not seen him, "...since that Sat'day shootin' at the Rabid."

All the other occupants of the house were questioned, but Blakely learned nothing to help establish Leonard Bowen's true identity. It seemed the murdered man had kept himself to himself, with never more than a raised hand of recognition as he hurriedly passed other occupants on the stairs or in the hallway.

Bowen's room was thoroughly, but unproductively, searched. Hopes were hugely raised, however, when Blakely successfully lifted fingerprints from various items. Between them, a hairbrush, a cheap fibre suitcase, and the mug and kettle standing beside the solitary gas ring all produced excellent quality prints of several digits.

The Records Department at Scotland Yard had no match.

Despite extensive enquiries around the area, no further evidence was forthcoming. The case was never officially closed, but after some weeks no further resources were allocated to it.

Stanley Gilbert retired two years later, still bemoaning the worst failure of his career. In less than three years, he was dead.

In the 1930s, the pub and parts of the worst streets around it, had been the subject of an urban slum clearance scheme. This ambitious and necessary project was postponed because of the war. But in 1949, *The Rabid Dog* – now a broken-windowed empty shell, stripped of anything that might have been worth having – was finally reduced to rubble by a municipal wrecking ball.

With the scene of the murder gone, the case was all but forgotten.

CHAPTER 2

SIX YEARS LATER

Monday 22nd October, 1951

In the Mile End Hospital, Joseph Farncombe lay dying. Two bullets had entered a lung, and the doctors said he could not be saved. Indeed, it was a miracle he had survived at all after he had been shot.

Farncombe had been brought in unconscious, but some time later he had come round, and became aware of his surroundings. He also knew what had happened to him.

Barely able to speak, he whispered to the young nurse on vigil at his bedside, "Am I dying?"

Her facial expression was enough answer.

"I want a beak," he whispered.

Thinking he was struggling to say 'beaker', she tried to give him some water.

He raised a feeble hand and intercepted the glass as she offered it to his lips.

"No. A magistrate. Now. I'm beggin' you."

Staff Nurse Donaldson had vaguely heard of a dying deposition, but in the few years since qualifying she had never encountered a situation where one was called for. Farncombe's *in extremis* clinical condition, together with the piteous way he made his request, mobilised her.

Almost dropping the water onto the bedside cabinet, she spun round and slipped sideways through a gap in the screens around his bed. Running to the Ward Sister's office a few yards down the corridor, she simultaneously knocked on the door as she opened it, and urgently repeated what her patient had said.

Sister McKenzie nodded. "Has he got long?"

"The surgeon said an hour at the very most. That was half an hour ago."

The senior nurse stood up, her starched blue uniform whispering as she moved. "I see. Well, the police have been called, of course. I know Doctor Raymond is a JP." She checked the watch pinned to her breast. "It's coming up to eight. He's probably getting ready to open the chest clinic now. I'll see if he's here.

"You go back to your patient. Tell him we're fetching a magistrate." Opening a drawer, she took out a small notebook. "In the meantime, take down word for word anything he wants to say."

The nurse returned to Farncombe and saw he had lapsed back into unconsciousness. Within a minute – and as if sensing that help had returned – he surfaced again, and weakly grasped her hand.

"We're bringing a magistrate for you now," she told him. Putting the notebook down, she placed her other hand over his and applied some lightly soothing pressure, wordlessly reassuring him that he would not die alone. His hand already felt cold.

"He shook his head. "Be too late," he croaked. "I see you 'ave a notebook. Write this down." He drew some shallow, laboured breaths. "I'm Joseph Farncombe. The Rabid Dog murder, years ago. The man killed that night were Gordon Mcleish. The rozzers never found who 'e was. I know. I'm the last one left who knows. Tell 'em what I say. Gordon McLeish."

A paroxysm of coughing followed his sustained effort to speak, and Nurse Donaldson thought it was the end. Astonishingly, he rallied once more and fixed his eyes on her. "'Ave you got it, Miss?"

She gave him rapid confirmation. "Gordon McLeish. Murdered at the Rabid Dog. You're Joseph Farncombe and the only one who knows."

"Good girl." He was gasping now, fighting to expel every word. With his vital organs closing down, but driven by determination, he managed to finish his agonising speech. "Something else… it wasn't a woman dunnit. It was a man wearin' a dress an' wig. It's 'im…Allen, wot's done for me an' all…"

His voice diminished yet again from very faint to barely audible, but his lips were still working. Nurse Donaldson leaned in closer and heard him breathe out the name "Allen" twice more.

With another bout of coughing, this time producing a lot of blood, Farncombe lost consciousness for the last time. The new arrivals now converging at his bedside – the JP, the Ward Sister, and Detective Sergeant Torrance, were all too late.

Dr Raymond checked for a pulse and shook his head. He pronounced the patient deceased at a quarter past eight.

Nurse Donaldson unfolded the top of the bedsheet and drew it over Farncombe's head as Sergeant Torrance removed his trilby. The four stood in respectful silence for a few moments.

Holding out the notebook, the young nurse addressed the medic, whom she knew from working on the chest ward a year or so earlier. "He wanted you to witness what he said, Doctor, but when he realised it would be too late, he asked me to write it down anyway."

Dr Raymond made no move to accept the book. "I see. This gentleman is a police detective – he introduced himself as we were running up the stairs. I suggest we find somewhere quiet, and you can tell us everything. Is that all right, Sister?"

"Yes, of course, Doctor. You must all use my room." With a brisk 'off you go' nod for her colleague, she said, "I'll stay on the ward while you're away, Nurse."

Settled in Sister's office, Sergeant Torrance introduced himself again for the young woman's benefit and showed his warrant card. Opening the investigation, he began by asking for some clarification. "Before you tell us all about the deceased, Miss, can you explain the situation to me, please. I was called here because a man was shot in Griswell Road a bit after seven this morning – I take it that's him who's just died? I don't even know his name yet; nor yours."

All the necessary information was quickly supplied. "I'm Emily Donaldson, and yes, he was the Griswell Road victim. His name was Joseph Farncombe. Two bullets in a lung. The surgeon said there was nothing to be done for him."

Dr Raymond chipped in. "On that last point, Sergeant, I don't think there's much I can do for you, either. I was called to witness a dying deposition. But whatever Farncombe said, and Nurse Donaldson took down, I obviously can't attest to it second-hand. Still, I'd like to hear what he told her, if that's all right with you?"

Torrance agreed to the request. Both men looked towards the young woman again.

"He could hardly talk, except in a whisper, but he was clear enough, and the first part was all about that shooting years ago in the Rabid Dog pub." She carefully and accurately repeated all that Farncombe had told her.

"He was in and out of consciousness, but next time he came round he said he was shot by the same man – Allen – wearing a dress and wig. He said the name several times. Then he died and you arrived."

Having given the detail to both men, she now addressed the detective. "I remember the Rabid Dog killing, it happened when I started my training."

"I remember it as well," said Torrance. "I wasn't in this division then, but every officer in the Met was aware of the murder – and that it was never solved. If Farncombe was right about the victim and the gunman, no doubt the case will be re-opened, and hopefully with more success."

"Yes, it certainly made the news," said Dr Raymond, "and like you, Nurse, I wasn't here; I was working in St George's. I never realised until just now that it wasn't solved. It made the headlines for some time, and then wasn't heard of again. I suppose I just assumed the police had got their man."

He stood up. "Anyway, there's absolutely nothing I can help you with, Sergeant, and there will be patients piling up in my clinic whom I can help."

Turning towards Emily Donaldson as he reached the door, the medic thought to say something more. "Well done, Nurse; not a nice business to be involved in. All of which makes me think I should give you some advice that I'm sure the Sergeant will agree with.

"Don't tell anyone that Farncombe spoke to you. If anyone raises questions, tell them he asked for a magistrate, but died before I arrived.

Which is perfectly true, of course, and much the easiest story to stick to for that reason. Don't say more than that to anyone except the police." He emphasised his next words. "Not to your colleagues; not to your boyfriend; not to your parents."

He considered the girl more closely, now remembering that she had been an alert and efficient presence in his clinic earlier in her career. "I think I need hardly explain why?"

Intelligent eyes looked back at him before glancing at the detective, who was obviously of the same mind as the medic and would have given the girl the exact warning himself before he left.

"Yes, I understand, Doctor."

"Good. I'll speak to Sister."

With the physician gone, the DS explained what would happen next. "I've made notes of what you've told me, but you'll need to make a statement later, because although everything you've repeated is hearsay and not evidence, the names you've provided will be material to the new investigation.

"Thank you for your help, Miss." Sergeant Torrance rose and gave the girl a farewell smile.

***

Torrance found a telephone he could use in the hospital. He arranged for the police doctor and spoke to the local Coroner's Officer. His next call was to his Chief Inspector, who predictably instructed him to start enquiries around Farncombe's shooting.

In carrying out this standard order, the detective was hamstrung from the first. He discovered that the initial call for an ambulance had only referred to a man collapsed in Griswell Road, Stepney Green. There had been no mention of a shooting and therefore no mention of needing the police to attend. The original caller hadn't even been asked for his name.

Fortunately, he was able to speak to the ambulance crew, who mentioned that when they arrived at the scene there were two people standing around. This was quite correct. An elderly couple had tried to assist. But with no connection to the unfortunate man themselves, and assuming that he had suffered a heart attack, the anonymous pair had gone about their business even before the ambulance driver had turned off his engine.

The crew only noticed some blood as they were loading Farncombe onto a stretcher. Since he was still alive and speed was crucial, they set off for the hospital as quickly as they could, arriving within very few minutes. It was here that examination revealed the cause of the bleeding and the call to the police was made – bringing the Sergeant back full circle upon himself, having discovered nothing new.

It was a little after nine o'clock when

Torrance returned to his police station and found his boss. He reported on his lack of success with the ambulance crew and waited for his superior's reaction.

"Hell's teeth," grumbled the DCI. "If that doesn't take the biscuit and then put the lid on the tin, I don't know what does! We haven't got the manpower to make house to house enquiries on the off-chance of finding these witnesses, and you know as well as I do that people round there close up like clams when they so much as hear the word 'police'."

He could feel his blood pressure rising. "I'm knee deep in the Dwyer murder. You're involved in that too – in fact, aren't you supposed to be interviewing people today?"

Torrance nodded. "The chap from the abattoir's coming in when he's finished his shift." He looked up at the office clock. "Sawyer will be telling me he's here any minute now, sir; it's why I left off and came back."

The Sergeant wanted to be dismissed so that he could prepare for his interview, but the DCI hadn't finished bemoaning the situation.

"Inspector Stevens is completely tied up. I've got people off sick right left and centre, and now you come in with not just a fresh shooting, but links to an old unsolved one too." He made his decision. "No, this is all beyond us. I'm going to see the Super. Tell Sawyer to park your witness *pro tem* and then come back here." He strode out of the room, his annoyance obvious in every step.

Torrance quickly followed him, and asked the Desk Sergeant to instal his witness in an interview room when he arrived, with an apology and a brew until he was available.

To the Sergeant's surprise, his Chief returned in no time at all, bringing Superintendent Livermore with him. Torrance sprang to attention but was told to resume his seat.

"Give me what you've got," commanded the Super.

The Sergeant made a second short, but complete, report of what he had learned. His ultimate superior received it all with the weariest of grunts.

"I understand you've got a witness in the Dwyer case waiting, Sergeant. Deal with that and we'll carry on here without you."

"Oh Lord, the Rabid Dog murder," said Livermore when Torrance had gone. "I was a chief inspector at the Yard then, and not in the CID, thankfully. Everybody talked about that case for weeks. To start with, we all assumed it would be cleared up in a matter of days. After all, a woman shooter was hardly common. Bound to be picked up very soon, we thought. But then it all petered out. Poor old Gilbert. He was DDI at the time. Never got over the failure."

The Superintendent articulated the shortcomings of the situation for his subordinate.

"I've no doubt Torrance has done his best with it so far, but it hasn't got us anywhere – we've wasted time and we've got no leads.

"This Division can't afford to get a reputation of having unsolved murders, and because we haven't got the manpower it's likely that's how this latest one would end up.

"Worse than that, we'd be watering down our already hampered efforts on the Dwyer case to deal with this new shooting and the resuscitated old one that's been tied in with it. We could end up with three unsolved murders on our patch if we're not careful."

He made a pulling motion with his fingers at the squat black instrument by the DCI's elbow. "Let me have your telephone. I'm getting on to the Yard to see if they'll help us out."

CHAPTER 3

In New Scotland Yard, Detective Chief Superintendent Philip Bryce took Superintendent Livermore's call requesting help as his Secretary brought in his ten-fifteen coffee. If this murder came at a bad time for the local officers, it was also a bad time for C4, the Yard's newest Criminal Investigation Department. However, even without the connection to an old unsolved murder, the new shooting – in a street in broad daylight – was evidently a very serious matter, and he could hardly refuse to take it on. He recorded the scant details the Superintendent could provide.

Concluding the call, he gazed balefully at the papers almost overflowing his in-tray. He abandoned all hope of reducing the heap any further for the time being, and instead concentrated on the case which had just been dropped into his lap.

With his thoughts in order, he reached for his internal telephone and asked Chief Inspector Nunn to come and see him.

"H Division is asking us to handle a murder,

Jack," he said after he had greeted his deputy. "A shooting with links to the old Rabid Dog case. Who can you give me to take charge?"

"Strewth, the unsolved pub case – that's going back a bit! As for senior personnel, the answer I'm afraid is that nobody is free, nor likely to be for a while yet."

He outlined the officers' whereabouts and workloads. "The DCIs are out in the provinces. I estimate another week in the sticks for both of them, possibly more. All three DIs are engaged with at least two cases on every man's plate. And frankly, sir, they're all ones which it would be politically embarrassing for us to abandon or even defer."

Bryce grinned. "Well, if we're that stretched, there's always you to fall back on, Jack!"

The Chief Inspector was surprised by the suggestion but instantly co-operative. "Oh, of course, of course. I'm a bit rusty on the fieldwork front, inevitably. But if that's what you want, I shall certainly step up."

He gave Bryce a wide grin of his own. "Alternatively, there's you, sir!" He expanded his thinking. "And, with respect, if this is a combination of a cold case and a new one, then that's very tricky territory." His voice and features became faux doom-laden. "Could put our young department's outstanding reputation on the line if it's not entrusted to the most competent of hands."

Bryce roared with laughter at this blatant

combination of flannel and manipulation, but accepted that he had been neatly cornered by his deputy. "All right, Jack. I'm sure you could tackle it very well, but I have to take into account the effect on everyone's paperwork if you disappeared for who knows how long. I shudder to think about it, actually; my entire desk as well as my in-tray would be submerged in no time.

"You're right; I'll have to do it. Who can you give me as bagman?"

Nunn considered. "Constable Firth could be diverted, sir. At a pinch, Sergeant Lomax as well. They're both in the building now."

The previous year, Bryce had simultaneously been promoted to his current rank and given significant freedoms by the Commissioner to create a new department within the CID. Ever since, he had taken a personal interest in the appointment of new officers to his department.

"I saw Firth at interview," he said, "and I remember I was impressed. A tough start in life; a Barnardo's boy. But no self-pity and a lot of ambition to make something of himself. I haven't had dealings with him beyond that one encounter, though. First name's John, isn't it?"

"Yes. My opinion is he's shown potential already. Reminds me a lot of Kittow and Drummond when they joined us."

"Better and better!" said Bryce, pleased to hear these two favourable comparisons. "Send him and Lomax up, would you, and tell them we'll be on the road very shortly, so they should bring their outer gear with them. I may not need both – or I may want more. I'll have to see the lie of the land, and then make a decision."

Five minutes later the two junior detectives, hats in hand and mackintoshes slung over their arms, were climbing the stairs to the third floor. They had not worked together before and had seen little of one another in the office. Firth, a thin and gangly officer almost as tall as Sergeant Howard Lomax, confided to his colleague on the way that he didn't know what to expect, working with such a senior man.

Lomax told him in no uncertain terms that he was being given an opportunity. "At the rate Mr Bryce is moving upwards, it won't be long before he's promoted to Commander. Then he'll be permanently trapped behind a desk and never get out on a case – and you'll have missed your chance to have the experience."

He gave his nervous colleague a friendly smile and some helpful information. "The Chief expects everyone's participation – not just our presence. Always bear that in mind. See that you speak up whenever you've something to say, whether it's work-related when we're on the job, or informally when we're calling him guv instead of sir. Remember that, and you'll soon feel comfortable in his company."

They were standing outside Mrs Pickford's

door, Lomax's hand on the doorknob. "All in all, count yourself lucky, John, and make the most of it, is my two penn'orth!"

Bryce, already dressed to leave the building, welcomed his subordinates and shook Firth's hand, as he always did when working with a new man for the first time. He pulled some keys out of his pocket. "We're taking my car, gentlemen, and because we need to make the most of what's left of the morning, I shall start briefing you as we go downstairs."

He passed on all that he had received as they descended the three flights, adding a snippet of information from his past as the trio walked towards the big police Wolseley. "I was a DI in H Division for two years after the war. But the army didn't let me out until the Rabid Dog killing had been effectively abandoned, so I was never involved in it. Just as well, that case was like a gravestone for the detectives involved. We'll have to hope we make a better job of it this time around."

With the car sedately moving through the London traffic, windscreen wipers working to clear a sudden shower, Bryce told his men he would drop them where they both needed to be and shared out some tasks.

"Firth, you're going to Mile End Hospital to find the nurse who was at Farncombe's bedside. You can expect to hang around a bit until she can be freed up, but it's important we get her statement. Probably not evidence for the most part, but useful all the same. It's also important, for her own safety, that she doesn't speak to anyone else about what she was told. Torrance didn't say he'd warned her, so see to it that you do.

"Whilst you're there, find out about the *post mortem*. If it's imminent, you should go and observe. Collect all the personal effects from the deceased if the local boys haven't already done it. Take note that I particularly want you to bring back the bullets following the PM. When you've done all that, come and find me at Leman Street station."

Firth, sitting in the back of the car and recording everything in his pocketbook, gave the DCS a lively "Sir!" to indicate he had understood.

"Sergeant, you go to the scene of today's shooting. Should be easy enough to pinpoint the exact location by blood on the pavement; look around for shell cases, although I suspect there won't be any. And see who you can round up in the way of witnesses. Any sort of description of our shooter would obviously be helpful. Again, when you're done, come back to Leman Street."

The Chief Superintendent slowed down and carefully steered the big police car past a coal merchant's horse and cart. "Something else has just occurred to me. If Farncombe was right, and his killer was also the pub murderer, you should look out for a discarded shopping bag. I remember one of those was used before and was found nearby. It was thought that the original gun was a Walther PPK..." He broke off to manoeuvre the car again.

"How they deduced that I don't know. The gun was never found and none of the witnesses had even seen it. Lots of pistols have the same calibre.

"But anyway, let's assume it was a PPK for the moment. Although it's a small pistol, fit a suppressor on and the whole thing is the best part of a foot long and too big to hide easily in a pocket. That means the bag was necessary, rather than an extra bit of female window dressing. Helped to muffle the sound a bit too, no doubt. And if the pistol was an automatic rather than a revolver, it would also catch the ejected cartridge cases."

Bryce, who was very familiar with both the West End and East End of London, made good speed via Embankment, Queen Victoria Street, Bank and Leadenhall Street, before turning into the Mile End Road. He set down Lomax first, and Firth a minute later. Making a U-turn, he drove back to his former police station and parked outside.

Realising that this was his second visit to his old haunts in a matter of weeks, he entered the police station feeling it was becoming something of a home from home. He was greeted by a familiar face behind the desk.

"We're expecting you this time, sir," said a smiling Sergeant Sawyer, as he lifted the end of his counter to join the DCS on the other side. "The Super said for you to use DI Carr's office – he's off sick. I'll show you the way."

"Thanks, Sergeant. A couple more things, please. I need everything relating to the Rabid Dog case. I hope it's all to hand somewhere?"

"I believe so, sir. The Super has already ordered PC Hill to dig out everything he can find. I'll tell him to bring it to you in here." He showed the DCS into a tiny, cluttered office. "What else can I do for you?"

"I want to talk to anyone who was involved in that shooting. I know the DDI has since died; but I think there was a sergeant and maybe a constable involved at the scene. Do you know if either of them is still around?"

"Not long after the murder DS Blakely retired early. He emigrated all the way to South America, Brazil I think, and didn't keep in contact with anyone as far as I know.

"Constable Paine was the uniformed man who was first on the scene. He's still based here." Sawyer consulted his watch. "Forty minutes time he should be coming in at the end of his shift. I'll wheel him along to see you.

"Oh, and DS Torrance is ready to talk to you. He's next door right now – shall I send him straight in?"

"Yes, please do."

The Sergeant had one last thing to say. "Just so's you know, sir, the Super asked to be informed as soon as you arrived. I'll be doing that next and I expect he'll be along to see you shortly." With that, the Sergeant took himself back to his counter via the CID room.

Torrance arrived promptly, and warmly shook the hand Bryce extended as he introduced himself. Their conversation was brief, because the local detective could add nothing more to that which Bryce had already been given over the telephone by the Superintendent.

The Sergeant was, however, able to hand over the few belongings the dead man had been carrying. He shook a smart brown leather wallet out of an evidence envelope, together with five shillings and four farthings in coin, and a front door key. The wallet held three ten-shilling notes, and an identity card in the name of Joseph Farncombe.

Glad to receive this evidence, Bryce half expected that the Sergeant would now ask if he could stay to help the Yard team on the case. Torrance, however, wasn't showing the slightest interest. No doubt he was already very busy – as Livermore had mentioned earlier. But, thought Bryce, if one of his own officers had similarly found himself as the first detective at the scene, he would have expected him to make a request to stay on the case and see it through.

The lack of interest from the local detective intrigued him. He considered possible explanations as to why this might be, because at first assessment the Sergeant presented as a perfectly sound and committed officer. He decided that perhaps the strong stench of failure clinging around those involved in the old case meant he didn't want to risk being involved with what might turn out to be a repeat performance.

There was nothing more to discuss. The Sergeant was hardly out of the room when a knock on the door was followed by the arrival of a very young uniformed officer, carrying a cardboard carton.

"Thank you – Hill, is it?" Put it on the floor wherever you can find a space."

"There's another box as well, sir. I'll be back in a minute."

Superintendent Livermore arrived in Hill's absence. When Bryce had been attached to this division as a DI, the Super had been a chief inspector in another division on the other side of London. Apart from their telephone conversation earlier, the two had not previously had any contact.

Livermore glanced down at the prominent 'Rabid Dog Murder Papers' label on the large brown box Hill had just delivered and approvingly remarked, "I see they're finding the goods for you."

Taking a chair, he stabbed a finger in the direction of the box again and said, "That old case has been something of a stain on the reputation of this Division; it would be grand if we could finally close it now. But I must say, I hadn't expected you to come yourself, sir. It's very good of you!"

Bryce's expression and voice were wry. "I came mainly because, like you, all my ranking officers are completely tied up on other cases. I've brought a new DC whom I've never worked with before and backed him up with a tried-and-tested DS."

"Well, if there's anything you need, sir – uniformed people, for instance – you only have to ask and we'll do our best to fix you up. And the Desk Sergeant will always organise tea or coffee for you all."

The fact that the Superintendent offered only 'uniformed people', with no mention of detective support, was not lost on the DCS. With his visitor soon gone, he was left to reflect on how it must feel for an obviously competent senior officer in his fifties to have to address a man, fifteen or more years his junior, as 'sir'.

No different, he supposed, to the situation in the army where grizzled warrant officers had to address newly-hatched subalterns in the same manner. He felt glad that, so far, he had never been in a similar position himself.

Turning his thoughts back to the case, he took out his penknife and cut through the string on the carton of papers, just as Hill arrived with another.

"That's the lot, sir. Says on the lid that this one's got the two bullets, and the shopping bag someone found in the street." The Constable acknowledged the thanks he was given and left.

Bryce immediately sliced through the string of the second carton and dug out a small pill box holding the bullets. He put this into his pocket without unsealing it. A quick glance at the bag told him there was nothing of value to see, although he noted it also held a scorched towel, no doubt used for additional noise attenuation.

There were no cartridge cases in the boxes, and no mention of them in the police notes. The DCS surmised that they had been caught in the bag, and the killer had removed them before dropping the bag in the street. He had then probably dropped the bits of brass into the nearest street drain.

Turning back to the box of papers, he lifted the files out onto the desk and began by reading the witness statements. That didn't take long, and he was none the wiser when he had finished. He moved on to the sequence of formal reports made by the former DDI and his Sergeant. These were far more extensive documents, especially in the early stages of the investigation. The obvious decrease in confidence in the later, much sparser reports, made for uncomfortable reading.

There were additional statements from various other people, the most significant of which was from Eric Mannington, the owner of the tenement building where the victim had rented a room. Overall, he found nothing which added to the anecdotal stories he had heard six years ago.

The identity card was next for his attention. Moving it through his handkerchief as little as possible, he inspected it closely, appreciating its convincing quality. He put it into a small envelope which he dropped into his pocket to join the bullets. Then he sat back to think.

If the first victim's real name was indeed Gordon McLeish – and the word of Farncombe was uncorroborated on this point – why was he carrying a forged identity card in the name of Leonard Bowen?

How did he know where to find the forger?

And above all, what was the nature of the criminality – or threat to himself – which would make him meet the costs of his fake ID, as well as the costs of the inevitable intermediary?

Something else which perplexed him was that there was nothing in the evidence boxes to suggest anyone had attempted to trace the originator of the false document. Finding the forger might have produced valuable leads. It seemed extraordinary to him that this had not been done.

Nor could he see that there had been any real effort to raise enquiries in other parts of the country about the victim's identity. All of the 'Removed To' sections of the forged ID had London addresses – each one a real, bombed-out street. Yet all of the addresses were recorded by Gilbert's men as having a non-existent house number.

For no good reason that he could see, the investigating team seemed to have tacitly accepted quite early on that because the man had a list of false addresses in very disadvantaged areas, and had quite recently started drinking in one of the seediest public houses in yet another poor location, he must have been local.

Bryce tried to attribute some logical explanation to this. The best he could come up with was that the Rabid Dog was hardly the sort of place a tourist would stumble across, much less choose to patronise several times a week. Regardless of that, the DCS felt more of an effort should have been made to establish where 'Leonard Bowen' had come from.

He made a note of previous missed opportunities and then looked at his watch. PC Paine should have appeared quite some time ago. Needing to stretch his legs, he wandered down the corridor to find Sergeant Sawyer.

The Constable's failure to materialise was explained with an apology from the desk man for not passing on the information sooner. Paine had returned to the station as expected, but was nursing a raging toothache. It started two days ago, but he had tried to ignore it. By the time he presented himself to his Sergeant at the end of his shift, the side of his cheek was swollen and he was having difficulty speaking. Sawyer had immediately made an emergency dental appointment and sent him straight off.

"Shouldn't be surprised if he isn't flashing all new gnashers at us when we next see him, sir," laughed the Sergeant.

"I hope not," said Bryce, alarmed at the suggestion. He remembered a great aunt telling him through ill-fitting and clicking dentures, that her first full set of false teeth had been a twenty-first birthday present from her parents, who believed that a crooked-toothed smile would be an impediment to marriage.

"I'd like to think our new National Health Service dentists would honour the third part of the Service's charter: to deal only with that which actually needs attention!"

He told Sawyer he would make time to see Paine whenever he returned to duty and went back to his temporary office.

CHAPTER 4

Sergeant Lomax had no trouble finding the scene of the murder and was soon squatting and peering all around. The earlier rain had left the pavement glistening wet, with the remaining blood dispersed and not particularly noticeable. He also noted that the camber of the pavement towards the kerb was relatively steep, with a large drain in the road nearby. Finding no trace of either shell case, he didn't discount the possibility that both had already been swept into the sewers. Or, if a shopping bag had been used this time too, then they had never reached the ground at all.

Whilst engaged in his hunt, a number of people passed the plain clothes Sergeant without comment until a perky little voice spoke from behind him.

"'Ere mister, what you doin'?"

Still on his haunches, Lomax swivelled round to face his inquisitor. The boy couldn't have been more than nine, but he had the slightly wizened appearance of children who have already lived hard lives. His shabby clothing and worn-out boots – the sole of one ready to part with its upper at the toe – confirmed the impression.

Standing up, Lomax deliberately moved within arm's reach of the lad and told him, "I'm a truant officer looking for boys who've bunked-off school."

The child started off like a greyhound from the trap. Lomax, quicker still and with the advantages of superior height and reach, anticipated not only his attempted flight but also the direction he would take, and successfully grasped him.

"Oh no you don't, you little rapscallion!"

The boy wriggled and writhed but was unable to slip the detective's hold.

"You tell me what you're doing wandering the streets in school time, and I'll tell you what I'm doing. But first, you have to promise not to run away when I let go of you."

"You ain't no truant officer?"

"No."

"Orlright. Promise." He was as good as his word and stood obediently. "I'm allowed to be late if my Nanna 'as a turn. School knows. I've had to fetch 'er Woodbines this mornin' to save 'er gettin' dressed an' goin' out."

"That shop there?" asked Lomax, inclining his head towards the newsagent tobacconist that he planned to call on when he finished his search.

"Yeah. They know the ciggies are for 'er." The boy, now at complete ease in the Sergeant's company, casually hooked his thumbs into the pockets of his shorts and advised him, "I don't smoke meself."

Lomax was stunned by the gaping contradictions between what he was seeing and hearing, particularly the extraordinary swaggering from a nine-year-old posturing like a hard-bitten youth ten or more years older. If it was all true, the boy was looking after an elderly relation, running her errands and skipping school. Absolutely ripe for falling into bad company and into trouble.

Shrewd little eyes clamped onto the Sergeant's, watching that he wasn't cheated out of their bargain to exchange information.

"Your turn now, mister."

"I'm a detective. There was a crime here this morning and I'm looking for evidence."

"Corrrr! You a good detective, are ya?"

"Good enough to know that you've just lied to me because you haven't got any cigarettes on you. And good enough to know that you wouldn't need to run from a truant officer if what you said was true!"

Lomax, pre-empting a second escape bid, had a hold of the boy long before he had finished speaking. "I'm giving you a choice," he said firmly to the little scruff at the end of his arm, "and it's one or the other. You tell me where you live; or you tell me where your school is."

"St Michael's," came the sullen reply, from

which Lomax deduced the boy had less to fear from his school than he did from his grandmother.

"I don't know it, so you'll have to take me there."

Not at all pleased with this diversion in his day, Lomax nevertheless felt that it was absolutely necessary. If he saw a bobby on the beat, he would immediately relinquish his responsibility. In the meantime, he loosened his hold and offered the boy his hand instead, a little surprised by how unhesitatingly a grimy paw was placed into it.

"I'm Sergeant Lomax. What's your name?"

"Vinnie – Vincent – Walker."

"So, Vinnie, did you lie to me about your Nanna as well?"

"Nah; not all of it. I do 'ave to do fings for 'er. Lots of 'em. Today she got me up early to go for the fags – said she was gaspin' and couldn't wait. I took 'em back to her an' had me bread an' dripping. When it was time for school, I went for another little wander."

Lomax pulled back his cuff and checked the time – a minute past eleven o'clock. If it was true that he went for the cigarettes 'early' before school, the child's 'little wanders' had kept him out on the streets for hours, with just a break for breakfast.

"Me Mum and Dad was killed in the war," said the boy, now happy to be in the Sergeant's company and inclined to chat. "I was just a little kid then," the swagger was back in his voice. "I never knew 'em. An' we lost their photos when we was bombed out."

"Sorry to hear all that," said Lomax, genuinely unhappy for a child who had experienced so much loss at such a young age. They rounded the corner and turned into another road.

"Yeah, it's 'ard. But I like to imagine them bein' here sometimes. Y'know, both alive. I'll see a man or lady in the street – like I did today – an' say to meself, you could be my Mum, cos Nanna said she had long blonde hair, too."

Lomax stopped dead, inadvertently yanking Vincent backwards. "You saw a lady with long blonde hair today? Where we were, back in Griswell Road?"

"No, not there. Here. In Frosdyke Street. I'd got the fags an' was goin' home." He pointed to a turning further ahead, indicating his home was in the adjoining street. "She come past me, real quick."

The Sergeant scanned the unfamiliar road, noting its curve and the tributaries joining it from both sides. He was an Oxfordshire man himself and had not lived long in London, but he knew that tons of bombs had been dropped on the East End. The evidence that this area had been badly hit was all around him. Of the buildings still standing, he could pick out the soaring gables of a typical Victorian school towards the bottom of the street – he assumed this was St Michael's – with what looked like a mixture of small factory and industrial premises dotted in between.

"Did you see which building she went into?"

"She never went in no building. She got into a dark green van."

The importance of this information, and how it might so easily have been lost to him had he simply shooed the child away, struck the Sergeant quite forcefully.

He faced the boy and sat on his haunches. Lightly resting his hands on the lad's shoulders, his voice was slower and heavier when he next spoke. "Vinnie, you've lied to me once already. Tell me truthfully, did you really see that lady?"

The boy nodded. Taking hold of Lomax's hand again, he led him a little way further down the road before stopping outside some old livery stables.

"Here. This is where the van was parked."

The Sergeant felt he had no reason to disbelieve the boy and every reason to accept what he said. He had one more question, and quickly devised a little experiment to help him arrive at the answer.

"All right, young man, I need you to do something. I'm going to stand right here, where you said the van was parked. I want you to go back up the street and stand at the point where you were when you saw the lady get in the van and drive off."

"No! No!" The child was swinging his head from side to side.

Lomax, astonished by this unexpected withdrawal of co-operation, questioned him rather sharply. "What do you mean, no? Why ever not?"

"Oh, I'll go up the road for yer orlright; 'course I will. All's I meant was no, she never drove off. She climbed in the back of the van."

The thumbs were back in his pockets and the beyond-his-years swagger returned. "Fought it was a funny way to treat a lady meself, makin' her go in the back of a van if you've got seats in the front. I wouldn't do that to my Mum. So I had a look as I passed. No one in the front at all.

"But I sez to meself, maybe she was waitin' for some men to arrive and take the front seats." He swaggered again, eager to share his observations and impress the Sergeant with his self-accumulated knowledge. "Men gen'rally go in the front, I've noticed, an' they're the ones who drive an' all.

"I took the fags to me Nanna," he pointed to the first turning on the left again, now only a few yards ahead. "When I come back later, to go to the park in Orson Street for a bit, the van's gone." His finger showed the opposite side of the road as the route to the park, a turning towards the top of Frosdyke Street which they had already passed.

Lomax realised his little experiment was redundant. Having wrongly assumed that the shooter had driven off immediately, he had intended to gauge whether the child was at a distance to read any of the numberplate before even asking him if he had done so. Instead, alternative questions needed to be asked.

"So, you're telling me you walked all the way up *to,* and then *past,* the green van, Vincent. Just to look inside? Is that what you're telling me?"

"Yep. No one in the front. When I come back the van's gone. I didn't stay long in Orson Street 'cos the Parkie there is 'orrible. Won't let me play on the swings or collect conkers, an' they're really good this year."

"Since then, you've been wandering around until you saw me – even in the rain?"

The boy nodded. "I didn't get wet cos there's old bits of bombed buildings to dive into everywhere."

Lomax, already concerned at the risks the child was running, added 'buried under falling masonry' to the list.

Vincent was still explaining. "I was on me way back to school meself – to get me milk an' free dinner – when you caught me. Dinner's the best thing about school."

Suddenly the spark and liveliness seemed to go out of the child. "Reckon I've just twigged what yer really after, mister. It's the van's number, innit?" He nodded sagely to himself. "Never looked at it. Never been int'rested in them the way some kids are." He looked up at the Sergeant dejectedly. "But it was an old Singer Bantam, if that's any good to yer? Wiv no writin' on the side of it. Just plain green."

Lomax took the boy's hand again. Beaming down at him he said, "It's a *lot* of good to me, Vinnie, it really is. You've been an absolute diamond, and if I had a little medal I'd pin it right here," he lightly tapped the lapel of the boy's thin jacket. "And that's exactly what I'm going to tell my boss at Scotland Yard, and your Headmaster."

He quickly exchanged his smile for a serious expression and voice. "But I don't *ever* want to hear you're bunking school and roaming the streets again. I'll be checking up on you, Vinnie."

The child, hopping about on the spot in sheer delight at the warmth of the Sergeant's initial praise and the mention of an imaginary medal, was even more overjoyed at his promise to maintain contact.

"Will yer really check up on me, mister? Come an' see how I'm doin'? Cross yer heart an' hope to die, will yer?"

Realising the boy had perhaps elevated him to a surrogate father figure, Lomax answered carefully. He had no intention of making promises he could not keep, but at the same time knew that he would like to see the little ragamuffin stay safe and not slip back into bad habits. "Yes; and I'll be talking it all over with your Headmaster."

They had arrived at a pair of old iron gates. The school secretary, spotting them through her office window, came to unlock the big padlock. Swinging the gate open a fraction, she moved aside. In stony silence, and giving Vincent a stern old-fashioned look, she clearly intended to admit only him and not the Sergeant.

A quickly produced warrant card ensured that Lomax was soon seated in the Headmaster's office, Vincent whisked off by the secretary to belatedly join his class and drink the bottle of milk waiting for him.

The Head was quickly appraised of the morning's events, and in return Lomax learned a little more about the tragedies in the boy's young life. Although doubly unfortunate in losing both his parents, the child was apparently far from alone in what he had experienced, with several more orphans in the school and an even greater number of children fatherless.

Within fifteen minutes, the Sergeant was walking back towards Griswell Road to resume his investigations, arrangements having been made to question Vincent again in school, if needed. He had also accepted an invitation to return at his convenience to give a talk to the older children in assembly, thinking that it would be an ideal first way of proving that he intended to keep his word to maintain contact.

Back at the scene of the shooting, Lomax decided there was nothing to gain in continuing his shell case search. He had almost been at the point of giving up when Vincent had arrived anyway, and he now headed straight for the newsagent tobacconist, observing above the front door that the proprietor's name was James Porter.

He entered what might have been any one of a hundred or more similar shops in London alone, mostly run as one-man enterprises, usually with a wife to spell the owner when a break was needed, or to help when the shop was extra busy.

The interior was small, and characteristically laid out. A revolving self-selection newspaper rack was parked just outside the door under the awning, with a fixed magazine rack against an inside wall. A glass-topped counter displayed an assortment of confectionery beneath, only accessible from the shopkeeper's side. One portion of the shelving behind the counter held a few bottled sweets, but by far the largest area was taken up with everything a smoker – whether cigar, pipe, or cigarette – could possibly want.

There was only one customer at the counter, asking for half an ounce of tobacco and some rolling papers. When he had been served Lomax moved forwards, warrant card in hand. The shopkeeper, a small man in his forties with the worst cough the Sergeant thought he'd ever heard, looked dubiously at the card and asked a one-word question.

"Yeah?"

"I hear you sell tobacco goods to young children, Mr Porter. If I ever learn you've done that again I shall nick you." Lomax waited for a response. A flat denial wouldn't have surprised him, but the shopkeeper didn't bother to lie.

"I sells to the one kiddie, and only the one. Vinnie Walker." His tone and manner were aggrieved, as though affronted that solitary breaches of the regulations should carry any consequences. "An' I know he takes 'em straight to his Nanna because she sometimes comes in herself. She swears he never touches 'em. Says the pack arrives as full to her as when it's left me. Always."

Porter had not finished standing on his misconceived dignity. "You've got pubs hereabouts that you police lot should be taking a look at. Filling jugs with beer and who knows what else for the kiddies. Never you tell me that all gets home and not a drop drunk on the way!"

"I might well visit them. Still illegal, what you're doing though," persisted Lomax. "I'm looking the other way this once because I'm here for another reason. But like I said, no second chances." He pulled out his pocketbook. "What can you tell me about earlier this morning?"

"This morning?" Deep furrows appeared on Porter's brow. He puffed his cheeks out and took his time arriving at what the Sergeant wanted. "You mean the geezer who collapsed on the pavement?"

"That's it. Did you see what happened?"

Another frown and a genuinely perplexed answer. "Yeah. But next to nothing to see. Sort of thing that's probably happened loads of times already today in London, as well as up and down the country."

"I need to hear about it just the same. All of it. Start to finish."

"Suit yourself," said the tobacconist, not even trying to understand why the morning's events – all clear enough to him at the time – could possibly be of interest to the police.

"I'm a creature of habit. It was maybe quarter past seven and I was standing in my doorway having a smoke and a look at the day outside. My last two customers had just left and were walking up the road together. Slowly, cos they're elderly. I notice there's a chap a bit ahead of 'em – and don't bother to ask me who 'cos I didn't recognise him. All I know is he didn't come in the shop. There's a lady walking the other way. No idea who she is, and she didn't come in the shop neither.

"Next thing, this other woman, all blonde hair and in a hurry, has already passed me by and I'm looking at the back of her walking really quickly up the road. She overtakes the Collisons first, then starts catching up the other chap. She's ploughing along. Head down as if she's walking into a strong wind, her frock and cardigan flapping."

"What colours?"

"Colours?" Porter was stumped.

"Yes. Of the frock and the cardigan"

"Dunno really. Call it dark, with some bright..." he waved his hands in small circles "...

sort of splashes of light colour on the dress. The cardigan was light, not dark." He hesitated. "Or maybe it was dark not light. I forget."

"Never mind. Go on."

"That's when I look the other way, for a bit of a change of scenery. When I look back up the road again, I see the geezer stretched out on the pavement and the Collisons doing what they can to help. I see he's not moving, and he must have been down for a quite few seconds by that time cos he's 'ardly any further forward than the last time I looked. The blonde woman's gone, so she's no help and she obviously didn't see any of this 'appening."

Lomax didn't interrupt to correct the tobacconist's misunderstanding of events.

"I know the pavement isn't the place for him if he's had a heart attack, so I put my head into the bakery next door an' tell Charlie – he's got a telephone. He rings for an ambulance. Then I shout out to let the Collisons know what I've done."

"Mr and Mrs Collison, do you know where they live?"

Porter gave the address before asking, "What's the big deal with this chap then; he all right?"

"'Fraid not. Shot twice. Died in hospital soon after."

"Shot dead?" Porter's eyes were swivelling in his head as he tried to reassemble in his mind what he had seen. He came to the correct conclusion but seemed incapable of accepting it. "By that woman? Up the road here? Never!"

"That's what we need to find out. Thanks for your help, Mr Porter. Someone will be along to take your statement, but if you think of anything else in the meantime, contact Leman Street police."

Out in Griswell Road once more, Lomax checked his watch. It wasn't quite mid-day, and he was very pleased with the progress he was making. Following the directions Porter had given him, he easily found the Collisons' house and knocked on the door. It took a while before a bent little man answered his knock.

The Sergeant introduced himself and explained the need for his visit. He was soon sitting in a comfortable living room, fussed over by Mrs Collison, who had appeared from the kitchen in response to her husband's call, already carrying a pot of tea to wash down their recently finished lunch. She brought another cup for Lomax.

With a cup and saucer balanced on the arm of his chair and his pocketbook open once more, Lomax began by explaining that the man they saw collapsing had in fact been shot, and had since died. Both Collisons were astounded, and said they had no idea.

"Do you think the blonde woman did it?" enquired Mr Collison.

"It seems so. Let's go through everything you can remember about what you saw."

Lomax, recording the key points of what the Collisons' reported, was satisfied that all of what he was told tallied precisely with what the tobacconist had said.

He was particularly pleased when Mrs Collison was able to supply a better description of the shooter's clothing, her husband floundering at the question in much the same way Porter had.

"Her dress was a summer-weight one, navy blue with yellow flowers on it. Quite big sprays, rather nice. Her cardigan was yellow too, although a paler shade than in the dress – more primrose. She had a dark coloured shopping bag, as well, but not down by her side. She was carrying it quite funny, hugged up under her bosom." She demonstrated the strange position.

"That way round? You're sure?" asked Lomax.

"Completely. That's how she passed me. That's how she passed the man in front."

The couple were both clear on the way the woman had pushed up against Farncombe, Mr Collison describing her conduct disapprovingly. "It was rude and unnecessary. There was plenty of space on the pavement for her to pass him, the same way she'd just passed the pair of us without any pushing – and we were walking arm in arm."

Satisfied that he had all the information the Collisons' were able to give him about the assailant, Lomax had only one more question. "You were obviously about quite early this morning, was there a particular reason why?"

"Only the one," laughed Mr Collison. "As we've aged we've realised we're at our best first thing. Many older folk sleep less well at night, you know, and we don't want to rely on powders. So we get ourselves up and out to Porter's for the paper, and then back here via Dixons in Argent Street for any groceries. When we've had our early lunch, we take our naps to make up for our shorter night."

Lomax thanked them and said they would be contacted regarding making statements.

CHAPTER 5

On his return to Leman Street, Lomax reported the detail of his morning's investigations. Firth listened closely, hugely impressed at how much his colleague had achieved by himself.

The DCS was delighted. "Well done indeed, Sergeant! As good as we could have hoped for. We now have descriptions of our shooter's clothing and getaway vehicle. Although we can't say for sure that the woman described by young Vincent is the one we're after, it seems very probable that she is.

"Moreover, if the lad's description of passing the van, and Mrs Collison's description of the way the bag was carried are both accurate, I think we can provisionally conclude a couple of other things about our suspect as well."

Lomax had already thought about both of these conclusions. He grinned and raised his eyebrows at his junior, knowing that the DCS would expect the Constable to answer first.

Firth didn't take long to work out what the senior men had surmised. "If there was no one in the front of the van, it's likely our shooter was changing in the back before climbing into the front and driving off himself. Which suggests he's working on his own – no accomplice?"

"Exactly my thinking," agreed Bryce. "The van explains how Allen – if that's his name – made his escape even better than a car would. He parks the van in a quiet street round the corner from his target. He returns to the van in no time after the shooting. In the back, out of sight, he whips off the wig and probably does a quick change into trousers and so on. Then he climbs into the front and drives away. No need to race off,

"What about the shopping bag, Constable?"

Firth arranged his arms in the manner demonstrated by Mrs Collison and reproduced by Lomax – right arm across the body supporting the bottom of the bag, left arm above and inside the bag. "If his arms were this way round, and he passed Mrs Collison and Farncombe from behind on their left sides, then he's probably left-handed."

"Yes, either that or ambidextrous. Left-handed would be much more usual so we'll work with that.

"Lomax, just one thing: did you say – or even hint – to any of these people that the woman might have been a man in a dress and wig?"

"I didn't, sir, no. Should I have done? I thought you might want to keep that back for a bit."

"It wouldn't have been the end of the world

if you had, but it might pay to keep our knowledge under wraps for the moment.

"How did you get on, Firth? Obviously, the nurse knows about the disguise already, but you warned her?"

"Didn't need to, sir; she said the magistrate doctor had spelled out the need to keep quiet. There's only the two of them at the hospital, plus Sergeant Torrance, who know about the disguise. I took her statement."

"Good. I want everything we can get on record. What about the *post mortem,* did you see that and bring the bullets?"

"No, sir. It's scheduled for a quarter to six tonight, in the hospital mortuary. Shall I attend?"

Bryce pondered. "No, I have another job lined up for you, Firth, and it might run on. But what about you Sergeant; ever seen a PM?"

"Not yet, sir," admitted Lomax.

"All right, this one's yours, then. You'll get another chance, Constable, don't worry."

"Disappointed sir, naturally," said Firth, looking and sounding anything but.

Bryce had to smile. "No; it's not a pleasant experience, but it's part of the job. I've wondered more than once how some pathologists perform them every day, and still manage to keep their appetites at mealtimes.

"Speaking of which, after lunch I want you to go back to the Yard, Firth. Go to Records. Tell them you're working with me. Two jobs: first,

I want details about any known villains by the name of Allen.

"Our problem here is that we don't know if Farncombe was referring to a Christian name, probably spelt A-l-a-n, or as a surname – in which case it's probably spelt A-l-l-e-n, but don't overlook any alternative spellings. Rope in the most experienced records officer to help you.

"Our starting point is that a man who appears to be a professional hitman now, probably went off the rails earlier in his career and may have a record for far less serious violence.

"Ignore men born before 1905, or after 1930. Make a brief list of any others. I have no idea how many you'll find, but I'll be surprised if there aren't a fair few Allens in that age group.

"Your second, and hopefully more straightforward job, is to see what we know about Joseph Farncombe. It may be that he's purer than the proverbial snow, but for the moment I strongly doubt it.

"While you're doing all that, Firth, Sergeant Lomax and I will go and search Farncombe's home. I'm hoping that, on his deathbed, he didn't have any reason to lie about his name and that his ID is genuine. If not we're up a creek the same way our colleagues were with the fictitious Leonard Bowen, and we'll have to do a lot more leg work.

"When I get back to the Yard, my priority will be to make enquiries further afield – see if other cities have anything on an Gordon McLeish.

And with a name like that, I shall be looking north of the border first.

"But now, it's well past time for me to find some nourishment – what about you two?"

A loud growl from Lomax's stomach gave the DCS one answer, and Firth confirmed he had also not eaten.

"There's a café in the Whitechapel Road that I use when I'm out this way. Let's see what they can offer us."

CHAPTER 6

Bryce's café did the men proud. The three officers sat down and put away pies and mash, all covered in good gravy.

The tables were too close together to let them talk about the case, so much of the mealtime – when mouths were temporarily empty – was taken up with a discussion about the General Election, to be held three days later. Sergeant Lomax was open about his choice and said that he intended to vote Conservative. Constable Firth said he still hadn't decided, although from his various comments he clearly had a fair understanding of the policies of each of the two main parties.

The DCS was silent on his own voting choice. He had voted Labour in 1945, being in favour of things like the introduction of a national health service, and the nationalisation of the railways, together with the electricity and gas industries, and the coal mines. He was more ambivalent about other actions, such as nationalisation of the Bank of England and the civil aviation industry.

Previously, he had also been impressed by the Labour Leader, Clement Attlee. An ex-army officer and barrister like himself, and from a very similar background, he had done a decent job as Churchill's deputy through most of the war. However, Bryce couldn't help feeling that Labour had somewhat run out of steam – certainly they had lost a few of their most talented ministers through death or sickness – and that after six years perhaps a change of government might not be a bad thing.

After rounding off their meals with huge mugs of strong tea, the detectives dived into the nearby Aldgate East tube station. Firth took a westbound train to Westminster, while his superiors went two stops eastbound to Stepney Green.

Bryce remembered the street shown in Farncombe's ID card, and didn't need a map or to ask for directions. But before proceeding to his home, the detectives made a detour to the site of his murder, so that the DCS could take a look at the scene himself. It was clear that the news of the killing had already spread, probably via the tobacconist, because a bit of sawdust had been thrown over what was left of the blood after the earlier rain.

"I didn't speak to the man in the bakery who called for the ambulance this morning, sir. There didn't seem to be a lot of point, because it's not a retail shop with a big window onto the street." Lomax pointed at the building next door to Porter's shop. A tall chimney was pumping pleasant-smelling steam into the street. "It's a small enterprise, exclusively supplying bread and cakes to hotels and other shops.

"And I didn't find the shopping bag this morning, but someone might yet find it and hand it in."

"Always possible," agreed Bryce. "Although I doubt if it would help us any more than the first bag helped investigators years ago. I looked at the original earlier – exactly like hundreds of others in use around London every day. Something I hadn't heard before, though, was that an old towel was inside the bag, presumably wrapped around the gun to muffle the sound even more than the assumed silencer would."

Lomax went the few yards further to speak again to the tobacconist, while the DCS looked towards the shop, assessing the distance between where Porter stood and the incident. He was immediately satisfied that the event would have been plain to see for anyone with reasonable eyesight.

Turning, he was startled by a sudden flash of light. A few feet away, a photographer was lowering his big press camera and already changing the bulb. Next to him stood a bulky florid-faced man, dressed – incongruously for London – in loud tweeds.

"I wish you wouldn't let your cameraman do that, Jeremy," grumbled Bryce. "You should have the decency to give me a warning so that I can arrange my features more favourably for publication!" He could already visualise the headline in the following day's paper:

'Senior Yard Detective Dumbfounded By Latest London Murder'

Jeremy Grieves, crime reporter for a well-known national newspaper, scoffed away the rebuke. "Rubbish! It'll come out perfectly well, Philip. Matt here is the best, but even if he wasn't, I'm sure your admirers would settle for any old picture of you." He smiled ingratiatingly and fished for information. "So, on *this* occasion H Division has called in the Yard's finest. Bit of luck for me, finding you here, old boy."

"What do you mean, on this occasion?" queried Bryce, stalling.

"Come on, Philip. We hear from our contacts that a man was shot this morning, right there," he pointed to the sawdust. "And that the killer was a woman, whose description just happens to match that of the Rabid Dog murderer from years ago."

"I really don't know why so many people call you lot when they see something, instead of calling us," said Bryce, genuinely irritated by the fact. "You give them an inducement, I suppose? Whereas we just give them sincere thanks."

Grieves ignored this. "What about a statement, Philip? You must have something you can put out by now, surely. And since I'm the early bird on the scene, I think I should be rewarded!"

Bryce, who had hoped to avoid the press until the next day, weighed up his options. As far as possible, he liked to maintain an even-handed working relationship with the 'fourth estate', but he decided on this occasion to share a little of what he knew, in the hope that at some point in the future this small gesture of favouritism would be repaid by the journalist.

"All I can say is this. Yes, a man was shot dead here this morning. His name is believed to be Joseph Farncombe. And yes, witnesses indicate the killer was a woman. Whether there's any link to the old case you mention, it's far too early to say, and I certainly won't speculate on the point, Jeremy, just to give you some extra copy!"

The reporter, a keen member of his local amateur dramatic society, had a fine variety of facial expressions to suit different situations. He put on his most cynical.

"You must think I'm as green as I'm cabbage-looking, Philip! Apart from Annie Oakley, not many females have ever toted a gun. And even she didn't go around shooting people in the street.

"You're never going to make me believe it's not the same woman as did the Rabid Dog killing. Even the description of the mass of platinum blonde hair is the same in both cases. 'Like Jean Harlow's only more of it' was what our witness told us. Is there such a word as 'hitwoman'?" he asked rhetorically as an afterthought.

"I'm sure you'll print the word in your paper whether there is or isn't – and probably 'gunwoman' too," said the DCS resignedly. He changed his approach. "Jeremy, you really could help the police by letting us know if any of your witnesses saw the woman's face. So far, all we have are people who were behind her."

Sergeant Lomax joined the little group as Grieves was giving his obliging agreement to this request.

"I'll do that, but we haven't found one yet who saw her face. And believe you me, we're trying!" He scrutinised Bryce again and realised there were no more crumbs to be had. "Oh well, if you won't give me anything else, Matt and I will say goodbye and push on. We have people to talk to," he said, archly.

"I wouldn't be surprised if they follow us," said Bryce to Lomax when the pressmen were out of earshot. "Not that we can prevent them."

In fact, the detectives weren't followed and arrived at Farncombe's residence without unwelcome company. Situated in a street of small but decent-looking properties, many of which had been converted into flats, Farncombe's home was on the ground floor of a two-storey house. The key he had been carrying slipped into the front door lock and the detectives let themselves in.

The flat was compact but not cramped. It contained a living room, kitchen, bathroom, and a bedroom. The furniture and fittings were very serviceable and not of the cheapest type, although Bryce thought little of the decoration was in what most people would call 'good taste'.

This was especially true in the bedroom, where a large cork board displaying nearly nude prints, assailed the detectives. A copy of a recently launched American periodical, *'Modern Man'*, was on the bedside table. That the montage had been created with at least some material from this publication was confirmed when Lomax flicked through it and saw a number of missing pages.

The collage board, properly framed and suspended on hooks and wire from the picture rail above, was striking for another reason. It also incorporated many magazine and newspaper pictures of fully dressed young women, fresh-faced and innocent in appearance. Their advertisement straplines – promoting wholesome products and activities – had all been cut away, leaving only their faces and demurely-clad figures amongst the 'come hither' near nudes. A psychologist's delight, thought Bryce, to explain the seeming contradictions of the chaste and the carnal on display.

Lomax, standing by the board and noticing that the wire was crossed at the top, lifted one side to take a look behind. Carefully, he flipped the unwieldy board around to reveal the reverse. The subjects on this side could not be more different. Coloured postcards of national beauty spots looked back at the detectives, presumably for the benefit of the landlord or his agent, if they ever arranged to check the premises.

All questions of preferences aside, the occupier was clearly not poor and was able to live comfortably. A well-filled refrigerator in the kitchen – an unfamiliar appliance in most homes – was strong circumstantial evidence that Farncombe had a more than adequate income. Bryce was astonished to see two small tins of caviar sat on one of the shelves. Pointing these out to Lomax, he remarked, "I think our victim had connections to supply him with this."

The Sergeant, who had never sampled caviar but knew it was expensive and realised it must be hard to come by, grinned.

The discovery of a cash box at the back of a cupboard of tinned foods was of immediate interest to the detectives. Lomax counted the money, announcing that it totalled three hundred and forty-seven pounds.

"What's the betting this wasn't honestly come by, sir?"

"Can't see that any bookmaker would accept a bet on the honest toil option, Sergeant. But if you think it was, I'll take your bet myself and offer a thousand to one against."

"Tempting odds, sir," laughed Lomax, "but I think you know my answer!"

The detectives found very few papers in the house, the most significant of which was a copy of a tenancy agreement, dated eighteen months earlier. It was an unfurnished let. There was a current insurance certificate, covering the flat's contents, and some old bills concerning the gas, electricity, and rates. But there were no letters of any sort, nor was there either a diary or an address book.

After half an hour of thorough searching the DCS indicated that they should give up. Disappointed that nothing worthwhile had been discovered, Bryce went back to the kitchen and turned the key sitting in the back door lock. He inspected the garden, knowing from the tenancy agreement that it was included with the ground floor flat.

It was a small area, quite well-tended, with shrubs and beds bordering a central area of crazy paving rather than lawn. A large fuchsia bush was still in abundant flower in one corner, its purple and red blossoms dragging its branches down. A tiny garden shed up against the rear wall produced more disappointment when it held nothing except a few garden implements.

Bryce returned to the flat. Locking the back door behind him, he removed the key and placed it out of reach of anyone who, learning that Farncombe was dead, might try and smash through the glass to gain access from the rear.

"The fact that we've found nothing at all here suggests what, Sergeant?" he asked when he rejoined his colleague.

"He had somewhere else, sir. Somewhere he did business, probably well away from his home. A secure place to keep any goods he was fencing, and maybe his records. I can't believe he wouldn't have kept tabs on his 'goods in' and 'goods out', so to speak."

Bryce nodded. "That's my conclusion. He was obviously quite relaxed about his security here. Only one key for the front door and he even left the back door key in the lock. There's nothing here apart from the cash, and as valuable as that is, my feeling is it's a drop in the bucket compared to the goods he's got stashed away somewhere else.

"Pity we haven't found any keys which might open the doors to his hoards, wherever they're kept. He wasn't carrying any other keys this morning, and I don't believe we've missed them in our search.

"I'm going back to the Yard next. You stay. Take a note of the landlord's details and find out what you can about Farncombe. His previous address, and whether he leases any other property from the landlord.

"Ask the same questions around all the flats nearby as well, particularly the one upstairs. You may need to return this evening to catch people in. If you don't mind a bit more overtime, come back after observing the *post mortem*."

"Right you are, sir, I'll do all that."

The two officers split up, the DCS this time choosing to take a bus to Leman Street so he could pick up the police car.

***

Bryce stopped to speak to his Secretary before passing through into his office. "Any messages for me?"

Mrs Pickford shook her head. "Nothing important, sir."

"Good. Ask DCI Nunn to come and see me when he has a minute. And should you get any reporters calling about this murder case I'm involved with, you should pass them on to him.

"Also, call down to Records for me, please, and see if DC Firth is still there. I don't want him to stop what he's doing but let him know that I'm back."

Bryce threw himself into his chair and took out a small address book from his desk drawer. Leafing through a list of contacts he had assembled over the years, he found the name he was after. Before he could move his hand towards the telephone, his deputy appeared.

"Ah, Jack. I was caught by Jeremy Grieves at the murder scene just now. Someone had tipped off his paper. As soon as he goes to press we'll have every other newshound on the telephone or downstairs. I want you to field everything. This is our position." Bryce gave his colleague the same basic information that he had given to the reporter.

"I do think it's almost certain that today's

murder and the old pub killing were carried out by the same person, but for the moment our line is that there's no evidence to support the suggestion. Between the two of us, we have a little more than that, but we're going to sit on it for a while longer. Incidentally, Firth is shaping up well; for the moment I'm not going to badger you to provide additional manpower."

Alone again, Bryce picked up his telephone and gave the operator a Glasgow number. It took nearly ten minutes to reach the office he asked for, and a further five minutes before eventually being put through to the man he wanted – George Fraser.

Once connected, the two men greeted each other as old friends, despite the fact they had never actually met. Bryce heard that his Scottish counterpart had also been promoted since their last conversation and was now a Superintendent.

"Och, I might have known you'd still be a step ahead of me, Philip," laughed the Glaswegian. "But what can I do for you today?"

"You'll catch up soon, George, I've no doubt – and leapfrog me probably! As for what I want, it's the usual: information. About a man named Gordon McLeish.

"We don't have any record of him here in London, and I'm wondering, given his name, if you might have something on him on your side of the border. I can save you a bit of leg work – there wouldn't be anything more recent than 1945; he was murdered that October. Estimated age was between forty-five and forty-eight at death, so born somewhere around 1898."

"Gordon McLeish, eh? Hmmm...I'm travelling back in my mind to before the war now... but aye, the name does ring a bell," replied Fraser. "I'll get someone to take a look at what we've got, and then call you back. If I draw a blank, I'll enquire over in Auld Reekie for you, too."

Satisfied his request was in very safe hands, Bryce thanked his unseen colleague and wished him well.

Before he could do anything else, there were two telephone calls in quick succession – neither having anything to do with the present case. He dealt with those, and was interrupted again, this time by the arrival of DC Firth, who entered looking pleased with the way his afternoon was going.

"Come in and take a seat. Judging by your face, you've found something?"

"Yes, sir. Farncombe. He did have a record – back to 1924. Started off with petty theft and moved pretty quickly to burglary. Three prison sentences in the late twenties and early thirties. After which, he seems to have given up that career and become a fence instead. One conviction for fencing at the beginning of the war, but all quiet since.

"However, several officers have left notes in his file suggesting he was still at it – always managing to be a hop, skip and a jump ahead of anyone after him.

"There's something that doesn't add up, though. He wasn't being brought in himself, but last year, he grassed on someone. Doesn't seem to be to avoid taking a rap himself, reads more like he wanted to settle a grudge against someone. We gave him ten pounds for information laid. I've got the names of the three officers who've made entries in his records in the last two years, sir, in case you want to speak to them. One in H division, and the other two in K."

"That's all useful, Firth. What else do you have?"

"Records came up with one man called Alan as his Christian name – Alan Lapwood. He carried out the type of crimes we're looking at, but he's in his seventies now.

"Within the age range you set, we found six with the surname Allen. Three were definitely killed in the war. One's still a petty villain, minor thefts of various sorts and very recent convictions for them, too.

"It's the last two who fit your suggested profile best. Each had convictions in his late teens and early twenties for offences of violence: common assaults mainly. They probably served in the forces during the war, but nothing since then. There's no note to suggest they're dead, though. I reckon that's looking hopeful for one of them being our man."

"You carry on like this, Firth, and I'll

have you working with me again!" said Bryce approvingly. "Copy out those names and other details for me, please." He pushed a foolscap pad across the desk.

The DC transcribed the notes from his pocketbook and handed the pad back to his boss.

"I thought those tasks would take you longer, and I don't want to start any new jobs today. What about observing the autopsy with Lomax? I only need the one of you there, so you don't have to go."

"Oh, I know it's useful experience, sir. I'll do it."

"The first is the worst, but with Lomax there, you can always prop each other up if it gets unpleasant. Stop work now and have a break. Then get yourself to the mortuary in good time."

Bryce now had half an hour of peace and quiet. Fifteen minutes were spent clearing more paperwork from his in-tray, after which he put his feet up on the desk and leaned back in his chair, thinking about what should be tackled the following day. His mental scheduling was interrupted by the telephone bell.

George Fraser's smile was almost audible down the line. "Pinned down your man McLeish," he reported. "He worked with a gang of nasties before and during the war and garnered a few convictions for dishonesty. Right at the end of the war he melted away – or so it was thought. If he was your unidentified man in '45, then he didn't melt so much as get pushed off his perch. We have photographs of him, of course. I'll make sure you get the most recent."

"I'll do an exchange, George. We'll send you a set of the prints taken off the dead man in 1945. They should confirm things. Sorry; go on."

"If McLeish, a Gorbals man born and bred, went all the way to London, he must have had a very good reason for leaving not just his city but his country. More likely than not he upset the head of the hydra up here – Andrew Morton-Hugh, known hereabouts as the 'big yin' . That's the 'big one' to you Sassenachs. Not that he's physically big; far from it.

"Think of your vilest villain, Philip, and you probably won't come close to Morton-Hugh. He wouldn't flinch putting a contract out on someone for treading on his toe – never mind double-crossing him.

"He was given a twelve-month sentence very recently; regrettably the most we could get for the little we could prove against him. Very clever use of his catspaws – layers and layers of them, always obscuring the trail back to him. I'd like to tell you he's doing his time like a good wee convict in Barlinnie, but he'll be running his rackets from inside, for sure."

Fraser abruptly broke off the conversation. Bryce could hear him issuing orders.

"Apologies, Philip, back again. I'm going to pay Mr Morton-Hugh a visit and poke a stick into his cage. I'll admit that's as much for the pleasure of seeing him banged up for the first time, as well as seeing if he has anything to say – or any reaction to what I say.

"I'm also thinking I need to have a talk with Robert Rennie, known as the Weasel hereabouts. He acts as Morton-Hugh's number two, and when he's not in prison he's involved in all the dirty dealings for sure. We've managed to bang him away more successfully in the past, when it should have been his boss.

"But if Weasel thinks there's a murder rap coming along with his name on it, he might prioritise saving his own skin for once, and serve up his boss on a platter."

Another interruption was dealt with.

"I'll call you in a day or so, Philip, and let you know how things go."

Bryce was fulsome in his thanks.

"Och, no need," laughed Fraser. "Morton-Hugh has long deserved the gallows. He's the worst kind of mobster; slap bang in the middle of untold grief up here – of which we have a surfeit already without his antics. If I can show he commissioned the killing of McLeish that'll be just dandy. And drams all round on me afterwards, to celebrate!"

Highly satisfied, Bryce tackled his last task of the day. Contacting Superintendent Livermore at Leman Street, he put in a request, then decided to go home a little early.

CHAPTER 7

Having come to the Yard in his own car that morning, the DCS was spared the long underground journey he normally had to endure. Much as he and his wife loved their home, it was a fact that travelling to and from Brentham Garden Suburb by public transport was inconvenient and rather tedious.

The house was quiet when he closed the front door and hung his hat and mackintosh on the hall stand. Veronica, used to her husband returning home later, often much later than his 'expected' time, was delighted to see him arrive early, and observed that it was probably only the second time since their marriage.

With a kiss and a hug for his wife he asked, "How's our little cherub been today, Vee – not running you ragged, I hope?"

"Fleur is asleep, and looking utterly adorable in the way that only young babies can. Go up and take a peep at her now, darling, and I'll see about bringing dinner forward. Then we can eat and have a bit of time together before her next feed."

Bryce moved soundlessly up the stairs and silently swung open the nursery door. There was sufficient light in the room for him to look down into his daughter's crib. Small arms lay above her head, two balled little fists on the sheet. Tiny eyelids concealed her green eyes – very like her mother's – beneath a surprising amount of brown hair similar in colour to his own. He marvelled once more at the miracle of her arrival, and experienced again the strange sensation that Fleur had been with them forever already, although she was only five months old. Bending forwards, he planted the gentlest of kisses onto the ball of pink putty which was her nose, and then crept out again.

Returning to the kitchen, where Veronica had put a light under the potatoes and was rinsing cauliflower at the sink, he scrutinised his wife and asked, "Am I imagining it, or are you looking a little pale, Vee? I worry that you're doing far too much."

His wife laughed. "You're absolutely imagining it, Philip! I honestly think I've never felt better, but I'll be candid: I doubt I could say that if it wasn't for Lucy. She was a great help today, as she always is – with Fleur as well as with everything else I ask her to do. I don't think we could have found a more capable and biddable mother's help. When you next see Gerry Drummond, tell him from me to thank Anna again."

Turning down the potatoes to a simmer, she put the steamer with the cauliflower over the top of the potato pan. Veronica now needed to give her full attention to the rest of their meal. Sending her husband to relax in the living room, she put some lard into a heavy frying pan and started cooking the rissoles she had prepared earlier in the day.

After dinner, Bryce gave his wife an outline of the case he had decided to take on himself that morning. He hoped that Veronica, as she had done several times before, would produce some insightful comments to help him in the latest task.

"It sounds as though you're making good progress already," she remarked. "I've never heard of Constable Firth – did you appoint him?"

"Yes. We were trawling around for a couple of new DCs, and he applied. He was in uniform in west London somewhere. Although he had no CID experience, he shone in the interview, and I decided to take a gamble. Early days, but I've no reason to think he won't be a success, and already some good reasons to think the opposite. He's gone with Howard Lomax to watch an autopsy this evening. If he can stomach that he'll be up for anything!"

"This killer, Philip – you really think it's the same person in both cases?"

"Probably, yes. But when we recover the bullets from today's murder after the PM tonight, we'll get them to the lab with the original bullets – which have been retained. If they aren't too deformed, the comparator microscope will tell us if they're from the same gun."

Veronica offered an observation. "Men and women move differently when they run, Philip. I can't explain the difference, but I know that's right. If it is really a man in a dress and wearing a wig, someone ought to be able to say so."

"Unfortunately, none of the witnesses from either murder saw the killer run, as far as I know. Nor did anyone see his face." He laughed. "If we get a suspect, I don't think we could hold an identity parade, with him dressed as a woman and all the others in the line-up genuine women, and then get them to take it in turns to run past, to see if the witnesses could pick the man out by his movements! The legal objections to that would probably go all the way to the House of Lords!"

Veronica laughed with him. "I can think of a more practical problem. The parade would have to be outside if you wanted to test the running theory. You could hardly have your suspect free of restraints – and then tell him to run along!

"Do I get the impression you think the original investigation wasn't as thorough as it should have been, Philip?"

"I don't want to be too critical, Vee, but yes. There was no attempt to broadcast the details of the dead man across the country, with a picture. That might have produced an identity. Nobody seems to have tried to trace the person who forged the ID card, even though two or three were known to be operating in the London area at that time. And there was no attempt to find witnesses outside the pub who might have seen the murderer. One of those might even have seen him running!

"I'm going to see what Jeremy Grieves' piece says in tomorrow's Herald. It may be enough to get a few witnesses call in. In the meantime I've arranged to post a uniformed constable on today's spot in Griswell Road, with a free-standing sandwich board: 'Murder Here on Monday. Did You See Anything?' That'll be in place tomorrow morning for an hour either side of the murder time, and we'll probably repeat it for the next two or three days."

"Your colleague in Glasgow sounds like a good man, Philip. Do you think you'll ever get to meet him?"

"I'd like to, if I could find an excuse to go up there. I've never been to Glasgow, and George has never been to London. He's a few years older than me; served in the Navy during the war. He told me he never came south of Liverpool – not on land, anyway."

"I'd love to see some of Scotland. I know it'll be more difficult to travel with a baby, but maybe we could go up there on holiday in a year or so, and you could drop in and meet him."

Bryce said he thought this was an excellent idea, and the couple turned their conversation to other topics, chiefly related to their little daughter.

CHAPTER 8

On Tuesday morning, the trio of detectives assembled again in Bryce's office.

"Let's make sure we're all up to speed on developments," said the DCS. "Firth, have you given Sergeant Lomax an outline of what you found in Records?"

"Yes, sir."

"Good; we'll come back to that; but first, how did you two get on with the *post mortem*?"

The officers exchanged glances. "It wasn't so bad once you'd got used to the chemical smell," said Lomax. "What the Doc was doing was very interesting, and he talked to us quite a bit as he went along. I think he was glad of the company, because his assistant didn't say much."

"That's right," agreed Firth. "It was an experience, for sure, and I found myself feeling even more determined to find whoever shot Joseph Farncombe. Up until the *post mortem*, he was only a name."

This was an insightful observation, and Bryce felt again that Firth was very suited to the plain clothes branch of the Force. "I'm surprised that the mortuary assistant was a silent type," he said. "Every one I've ever met has not only been talkative, but well-equipped with gallows humour. I digress; carry on."

"These are the bullets, sir," said Lomax, producing a small box. "Point three-two calibre, was the Doc's opinion."

"Good. When we've finished, Constable, your next job is to take these, plus the ones from the Rabid Dog case which I have here, and go to Hendon. I'll brief the lab by telephone before you arrive."

Bryce produced the box of bullets from the drawer in which he'd locked them the previous afternoon. "Both boxes are sealed and clearly labelled – and I need hardly say that you absolutely must not open either one. We don't want some sharp barrister getting his client off the hook by arguing that evidence was compromised, or tampered with, by the police.

"This morning, I've stationed a uniformed officer at the murder site, trying to attract new witnesses. What we really want is the woman who Porter said he saw approaching in the opposite direction to Farncombe, and who would have had a better chance of seeing the killer's face. Of course, it may be a complete waste of time. She may have been in Griswell Road for the first and only time yesterday. Or she may only pass that way infrequently. But as always, we must try."

He next outlined what Superintendent Fraser in Glasgow had said, and the actions which were to happen in that city as a consequence. This produced optimistic reactions from the two junior men.

"Another very long shot, gentlemen." Bryce showed the false, Leonard Bowen, ID card. "The original reports said that good fingerprints were lifted from the lodging house – no matches found. But astonishingly, there's no mention that anyone tried to lift prints off this card. We can expect to see the victim's prints, but if we're lucky we might find some to fit the records of a known forger. When we're finished here take it downstairs with you, Sergeant, and put your powder over it. If there are any usable prints let Records have them.

"Also, ask Inspector James if he can give you the names of everyone at the time who could produce ID cards as convincing as this. It's a professional job which would pass muster almost anywhere, which means we're looking for someone at the top of the forgery tree, gentlemen."

Changing the subject, Bryce enquired, "Have either of you seen today's Daily Herald?"

The younger men shook their heads.

He took a copy from his briefcase, folded it and passed it across the desk. "Don't either of you laugh," he warned with mock severity.

The two officers inspected the photograph, which was actually not as bad as it might have been, although it had inevitably captured the look of surprise on the DCS's face.

"Come on, sir, you look fine," said Lomax.

Bryce grunted. "What about the story?"

The detectives read the short article, printed under a more favourable banner headline than the one Bryce had anticipated:

'Woman Shoots Man in London Street'.

The piece went on to speculate that the case was similar to the unsolved Rabid Dog public house murder six years earlier and reproduced some of the copy of the 1945 case. The new report implied – as good as stated – that the local police had immediately asked the Yard to take on the case in order to avoid the probability of another failure.

"Not much in it, really, sir," said Lomax. "But I bet the local Super is grinding his teeth and wondering if he can nail Mr Grieves for speeding. Or not walking in a straight line when asked. Or just about anything!"

Bryce laughed. "Yes, Jeremy's having a dig at H Division, no question."

"He hasn't managed to find out that Farncombe spoke before dying, though," said Firth.

"No."

"Nor does he know anything about the killer probably being a man," added Lomax.

"True, but I confess I'm surprised that he hasn't even floated the possibility to his readers that the killer could be male. I definitely want to keep that under our hats a little longer, hopefully to avoid causing our suspect to think we're getting close, and perhaps deciding to do a flit."

"That's assuming he's somewhere close at hand in the London area, isn't it?" queried Firth. "For all we know, he's hidden himself on his home turf already. And that could be all the way up with your friend in Scotland, sir."

"Also true," acknowledged Bryce. "But let's not depress ourselves with everything that might go against us – that's something which definitely dragged down the original investigation.

"In our favour, this report has now publicly linked the two cases, and that may help. Witnesses to the first murder might suddenly emerge. We shall see.

"When you've finished with the ID card, Sergeant, there's another job for you. If our killer is the professional we believe him to be, he's probably had intermediate commissions.

"We can't wait to put a notice in the next edition of the Police Gazette, so you should approach each of the big city forces in places where they have known gangland rivalries and turf wars. Manchester, Liverpool and Birmingham for starters, and anywhere else until you turn something up.

"Ask if, within the last six years, they've had an unsolved shooting where the weapon was a point three-two pistol. If so, we'll have to consider getting their bullets for comparison. Should they match either of our sets, the identity of other victims and their contacts may shed some helpful light on our cases."

Lomax nodded, his pencil recording everything in his pocketbook.

"Firth, after Hendon, start contacting those officers you mentioned earlier, the ones who made notes about Farncombe. See what you can learn from them. They may have names of people who used his fencing services. Maybe he diddled one of those even more than fences always do.

"That would be enough for someone to put a contract out on him in certain circles. But even so, I'm not losing sight of the fact that Farncombe knew Allen years before – and knew that he was the Rabid Dog killer. That suggests there's some other connection between the pair.

"I have a number of pressing matters demanding my attention today that I really can't delay any longer, so we'll all work independently. When you've finished everything I've given you, come back and we'll regroup.

"Questions, gentlemen? No? I'll see you later then."

CHAPTER 9

George Fraser had made the necessary arrangements in advance with Barlinnie prison. As he drove the few miles from his home, he considered his approach to his interview with Andrew Morton-Hugh. The two men had grown up together, but had seldom met since Fraser had joined the police. Indeed, since that point there was never a time when he hadn't wanted to pursue the 'big yin' for his crimes, and see justice properly done. This desire had even occupied his thoughts at times during his war service in the Navy.

Unfortunately, and as he had explained to DCS Bryce, Morton-Hugh was very clever and very elusive. The recent twelve-month term was the first handed down to him, and Fraser had heard on the grapevine that an appeal would be lodged imminently.

Parking his car, he was soon inside the huge prison and escorted to an interview room. Morton-Hugh sat at the table, a guard standing behind. Fraser took his seat and smiled at the prisoner opposite.

"Well, here you are at last Andrew, doing a nice wee stretch that we both know should have been ten times or more longer. But it's a start, and a taste of what your acolytes have been sparing you all these years."

Morton-Hugh looked over his old acquaintance. Even in his prison garb he was a handsome, self-assured man. Of rather less than average height, he exuded above average confidence to compensate, and sat at the table as though he alone was the authority figure in the room.

"Aye, well; good to see you again, too, George. It's been a while, as the saying goes. My lawyer – the one who's working on my appeal – told me you were personally instrumental in the miscarriage of justice that's resulted in..." he made an expansive gesture around himself "...my confinement here.

"You know, I've always thought it was jealousy with you, George. The old green-eyed monster eating away at you. We may have been born on the same day and started out from the same slum, but I've gone so far ahead of you I cannae even see you in the distance behind me."

His insolence was habitual. The hallmark of a career criminal who had built his reputation on his perceived superiority and invincibility. His eyes narrowed as he tilted back his head and looked down his nose at Fraser. "Imagine how hurt I was when you sent your wee minions to persecute me instead of arresting me yourself. Especially knowing how desperate you are to put me into a frame for something big."

He smirked provocatively. "But George, you havenae got something big; you havenae got *any*thing big. And when my lawyer gets my conviction overturned and my slate is wiped clean and my good reputation restored, you'll have had *nothing at all* against me apart from your falsehoods and your fabrications.

"I'll make sure your vindictiveness and failure are known to your superiors. I guarantee that very soon now you'll be begging your boss for a job back on the beat." He leaned forward and was almost hissing. "And I'll see he doesnae give it you, George. Like I said, I'm a leading Scottish businessman and you're jealous of my success."

Fraser listened throughout, betraying no sign of his strong desire to smack Morton-Hugh very hard in the mouth. "Aye well, we all know what they say about self-praise, don't we? And as for all your thoughts about me, let me return the compliment."

Grim-faced, he delivered an excoriation of his contemporary. "You're worse than the human excrement that still swirls around the gutters and the streets where we grew up, Andrew. Except that kind of filth is almost understandable when the only toilet in a building of forty people is blocked, and no one can find the landlord to do anything about it."

He glared into the eyes of the prisoner. "Your kind of filth is actually worse because it's inexcusable. Nobody chooses the misery and squalor of a rat-infested home – not that anyone can really call eight people living in one room a home. But you *choose* to add to that misery. And you drag others, who could escape it the way I did, right down into your mire. You're an obscenity, Andrew."

Morton-Hugh looked for all the world as though Fraser's contemptuous character assessment was a review of his finest characteristics, with a song of praise for his actions.

Feeling it was time to puncture his prisoner's arrogance and complacency and, if possible, extract a reaction to the information he wished to impart, Fraser told him, "You're quite right on one point though. I've *never* been able to make the big charges stick to you, Andrew, including at least two we both know you should already have swung for.

"And I'll no' deny you've been clever, buffering yourself with your expendable associates. But I've got this feeling now," he slowly tapped his forehead as though the feeling was arriving as he spoke. "I've got this feeling I'm overdue a lucky break.

"Imagine, I might pick up my telephone one day and hear a friend asking me for help with an unsolved shooting from a few years back." His expression became thoughtful, as if envisaging this lucky break. "Somewhere down South, perhaps. Mebbe all the way down to an old London pub, even?"

Morton-Hugh shrugged, completely unperturbed by the thrust of his old classmate's prophecy. "Not sure what you expect me to say about your little fantasy there, George, other than I'm pleased to know you've made a friend at last."

Fraser guffawed. The jibe was a reminder of the lonely life he had led in childhood, the charismatic young Andrew attracting their contemporaries – boys and girls – like flies to a honeypot. Or to a pile of ordure, as the Superintendent now preferred to view it.

When looked at dispassionately, the position of the man opposite him was hugely regrettable in many ways. Morton-Hugh had been an intelligent boy. A little leader, definitely; and charismatic with it. But one who ruled, as all bullies do, by keeping his young fellows in fear that they would be ostracised and victimised. Kept apart. Verbally mocked and physically knocked. All for not wanting, as Fraser had not wanted, to come under his control and dominion.

Morton-Hugh had soon graduated from his playground fiefdom and expanded, first into the near neighbourhoods and then the areas beyond. Despite his best efforts, the Superintendent still had no real idea of how far his malign influence had spread.

He stood up. "I'm done with you for the moment, Andrew, but I'll wish you a happy birthday for tomorrow. Mine will be celebrated in freedom and as much comfort as rationing will allow, with Moira and the family. And you'll be here, slopping out your smelly wee potty – just like in our old Gorbals days."

He stood by the door. Looking back at his former classmate he delivered his last few words with consummate derision.

"You're deluded if you think you've moved ahead of me. And I promise you this: lawyer or no lawyer, you'll no be moving out of here further than the condemned cell."

He gave another laugh and left his contemporary to be handcuffed and taken back to his cell.

Back in his car, Fraser knew he had gained nothing in the way of information from Morton-Hugh. Even his chilling prediction that the execution chamber was to be the gangster's ultimate destination had produced no reaction. He hoped, however, that behind the facade of untouchability, there was a worried man.

Although the interview had not produced any result, he allowed himself to enjoy a smidgeon of satisfaction as he drove along. Finally, and after twenty years, he believed he was a little ahead of one of Scotland's worst felons. His telephone had rung at dawn that morning, confirming his men had rounded up Robert Rennie. He was safely in a cell at Turnbull Street and ready to be interrogated whenever it suited Fraser.

Men had also been positioned to watch the Weasel's empty house. If, as Fraser suspected, Morton-Hugh was giving orders from inside Barlinnie, he anticipated someone would be sent, in person, to warn Rennie to keep his mouth shut.

The Superintendent's instructions had been to nab and hold everyone who turned up at the door, no matter how innocent-looking they might appear to be. This was an essential precaution, because there was no telling who Morton-Hugh's network of henchman could make use of, from the milkman to the grocer's boy, as a messenger. Only by rounding up everyone could he be sure that the gangster was kept completely in the dark until after Rennie was questioned.

Arriving at the station, Fraser checked with the Custody Sergeant that the Weasel was waiting.

"Aye, sir, he's waiting. Very unhappily."

"Good! He can fester another hour at least while I get some coffee and read my post."

The Superintendent enjoyed his coffee. He had made some additional arrangements at the station to ensure that Rennie was completely isolated. He had become convinced a long time ago that Morton-Hugh's organisation must include a number of serving officers, both in Barlinnie and the Force. He could not see how certain crimes could have been accomplished without inside help. These unknown individuals were either on the 'big yin's' payroll or at his mercy for some reason.

Fraser's extra precautions had included an order that a minimum of three officers were to be in attendance at all times to ensure there was no form of communication inside the police station from, or to, Rennie. This was an extravagant deployment of manpower, and not something he had resorted to lightly or without full consideration. He had gone further and spelled out to those involved why this increase of men was necessary: the policemen were to stand outside the holding cell and watch each other as well as the Weasel. The Super thought it was high time he let it be known that he suspected traitors in the ranks.

By the time the 'big yin's' number two was brought up to an interview room, Robert Rennie appeared to be trembling a little. Fraser correctly assessed this was mostly the effects of the chill and damp in the holding cells, but he also hoped that being starved of information and guidance from his boss might have contributed. Conversely, it was probably too much to hope that instructing his men to tell Rennie he was being brought in on a possible murder charge – without supplying any further detail – might have also rattled him up.

He opened the conversation solicitously, "Did they keep you in the cold down there, Robert?" before immediately applying pressure. "Or are you shivering because you know I'm itching to charge you with murder?"

Rennie said nothing.

The Superintendent pressed harder. "If you've any sense your teeth should start chattering now, telling me everything about a London shooting in '45." He paused, not expecting more than the indifferent shrug Rennie gave him, then added, "A Mr Gordon McLeish."

Trembles notwithstanding, Rennie was a hardened crook, practised in lies and deflections. Fraser, thwarted over so many years, sensed his time might yet be wasted in this interview. He moved to avoid this possibility by making a partially true statement.

"And I know a lot more than that, because I've already spoken to Andrew Morton-Hugh this morning. No matter to me if you'd rather not point the finger at him, because I'll be using what *he* told me, and charging *you* with McLeish's murder instead.

"So think on that, Robert. I intend to have the evidence for a conviction from one of you today. And if that means accepting everything your boss has told me as gospel, then you'll be making a trip to Barlinnie later today, and meeting the hangman in a few months."

The Weasel, deprived of communication and instruction, began to crumble. He knew only too well the lengths Morton-Hugh would go to. Left to make his own decisions, and faced with a capital charge, there was only one decision he could conceivably arrive at: how best to save his own neck.

A short negotiation preceded a torrent of information.

"I want to turn King's Evidence," said Rennie. He looked at the sergeant who was to take notes and pointed a finger at his face. "That's the first thing you write down and you write it down every time I say it. Then you show me that you've done it."

Sergeant Mair, selected for the speed and accuracy of his shorthand, looked at the Superintendent.

Fraser nodded to Mair in acquiescence, and the Sergeant showed Rennie what he had written.

"I cannae read that. It's not proper words!" protested the Weasel.

"Write that bit again in longhand, Sergeant, and show him," instructed Fraser. "Do it that way every time."

This satisfied Rennie, but before he could say any more the Superintendent spoke again.

"You know that the decision to allow you to turn King's Evidence isn't for me to make. The Fiscal will decide. All I can say is that if you make a statement which helps to hang your despicable boss, then I promise to back your application."

"Good enough for me, Mr Fraser," said Rennie, with all the resignation of someone who realised he had no choice.

CHAPTER 10

While the Scottish Superintendent was talking to his prisoners in Glasgow, Bryce was on the telephone to the Hendon laboratory, speaking to a scientist he knew quite well. The DCS explained about the bullets he was sending, and why the analysis was urgent. The expert agreed to expedite the examination, and promised that an initial report would be made by telephone that afternoon.

The morning passed; the DCS receiving and making various calls and speaking to several visitors. In between, he attacked his 'in' tray. He broke only to go to the canteen with DCI Nunn for a short working lunch of a sandwich, a piece of past-its-best seed cake, and a cup of tea. Afterwards, he returned to his office and picked up his clerical work where he had left off.

At twenty-five past two, Sergeant Lomax appeared and dropped himself into the offered seat.

"Couple of things, sir. The false ID was a jumble of useless prints, but Mr James gave me the names of two exceptional forgers. Problem is, one of them was given a five-year sentence in '43, so he couldn't have been around to make a card for McLeish in '45. The other man died about eighteen months ago. Literally a dead end with the both of them.

"The better news is that Leeds has an unsolved case. Nearly two years ago, a Liam Yeats was killed. Cause of death two shots fired from behind. Point three-two calibre bullets. The gun was never found.

"No witnesses – happened in a quiet residential street around midnight. Nobody heard the shots. The victim had form, and according to my contact wasn't a useful member of society. It was assumed he'd upset someone and been 'removed'. Enquiries got nowhere and eventually the case was abandoned. The Leeds boys say we're welcome to test the bullets.

"Oh, and Firth is back, sir; he's downstairs making calls."

"That's very good, Sergeant; and I absolutely want those bullets as soon as we can get them. We can't ask Leeds to pop them in the post because we have to demonstrate continuity with physical evidence. Arrange to borrow a uniformed man for a day. Fix it with Leeds that he's coming, then send him by train to collect them.

"If the bullets match ours, we'll have confirmation that our killer is a professional as well as a triple murderer – at least. What we're still missing in all three cases, though, is who did the victims' enemies contact to find such a murderous animal?

"While you're telling your counterpart about arrangements for collecting the bullets, ask if there's any possibility of questioning these rivals for information about hiring hitmen. We can't expect the same level of assistance I'm getting from my contact in Glasgow, but it doesn't cost us anything to ask for help. Come back here when you've done all that."

Lomax had only just left the room when DC Firth appeared.

"All sweet at Hendon, sir, and you should hear later today. Regarding the notes left in Farncombe's file, two officers gave me the same name – Samuel Palmer."

"Ah, I know him!" interjected Bryce. "Another burglar, until he got too fat to do any breaking-in – or rather, until he got too fat to do the essential 'entering' part himself. That's when he set up, for want of a better description, a burglary franchise. He selects a target and provides any specialist tools and advice needed. A member of his band carries out the job and pays his overlord, Palmer, an agreed fee.

"An ingenious scheme, in its way. Palmer never actually has the stolen goods in his possession, and there's never been any evidence against him. Nobody rats on him, because – it's said – he keeps a couple of heavies to enforce threats and break the legs of anyone who even looks as though they might be disloyal."

"You've got it exactly, sir; that's just about what each of the K Division detectives told me. Superficially, all of Palmer's burglars make their own arrangements for fencing their hauls, out of which they pay him. But one of the officers said he thinks Palmer runs it all a lot tighter than that. He thinks Palmer tells them where they have to fence the goods."

Firth, having had time to mull over everything the K Division officers had told him, advanced a theory. "Do you think, if word got back to Palmer that his little troop were disgruntled because Farncombe was cheating them, leaving them with less of a cut and making their enterprises uneconomic, Palmer might have taken action?

"He couldn't have Farncombe squeezing the life out of his golden geese, could he? All in all, Palmer sounds just the sort of man who might have an Allen on his payroll."

Bryce considered this. "It's not impossible, but very few 'heavies' would go as far as murder. So, while I agree that Palmer is someone we have to look at, I think if it was just a matter of appeasing unhappy burglar friends, and securing his own revenue stream, a simple beating-up of Farncombe would have sufficed. I think for Palmer to actually order the hit, it would have to be because he was more personally disadvantaged, or threatened, by something Farncombe had done.

"We'll definitely have him in for a chat in a day or so to find out."

Sergeant Lomax returned. "All fixed," he reported. "I borrowed a probationer constable. He'll go to Leeds first thing in the morning and take the evidence straight out to Hendon when he gets back. I've warned the lab people there's a third set of bullets coming.

"The DCI I spoke to in Leeds is going to talk to his boss about your request, sir. He wasn't at all unco-operative, but he did say they're overwhelmed with work."

"We certainly know that feeling ourselves," said Bryce understandingly. "In your absence, Lomax, Firth has come up with the name of a man who might have ordered Farncombe's death. He can explain all that when you go back to your office.

"What I want you to do now is start sniffing around the two Allens, but I don't want anything done which might alert our man if he's one of them. Delicate enquiries only, please, hard though that will be. We need to know where they currently live and what their apparent source of income is. Also, what friends and relatives they have, as well as any favourite haunts.

"Be a good idea to talk to detectives who've dealt with them in the past and see if they have anything useful to add.

"Oh, and I want copies of their photographs

from the files."

Within minutes of his team's departure, the telephone rang.

"Constable Rodway here, sir, from Leman Street. I manned the sandwich board in Griswell Road this morning and I may have something for you."

"I'm all ears, Constable."

"Several people spoke to me, the way people do, but none were any use. Until a lady came up and said she thought she must have seen the murderer, although at the time she didn't know anything had happened, or that anyone was dying. She couldn't stop earlier, but she's with me in the station now, sir. Will you speak to her?"

"Absolutely, Constable, put her on the line."

Seconds passed before a cultured voice reached Bryce's ear.

"Good afternoon, Chief Superintendent, I'm Doctor Victoria Metcalfe. It's possible I may be able to help with your investigation.

"I was walking to my surgery as usual yesterday morning. There were a few people about, as there always are, but the pavement was far from crowded. I saw a man approaching in line with me – we were both walking closer to the roadside of the pavement at that point, and I suppose I thought we would both automatically move aside a little as we neared each other.

"But before he could do that, a woman appeared from behind him – moving faster than he was. She was on his left as they came towards me. That's when the man suddenly stopped, and I had to sharply move further towards the kerb on my left to pass him. I have to admit I didn't look at him as I passed, because I could see a lorry rumbling up, and was more concerned not to step off the edge of the pavement and into oblivion under its wheels.

"I had no idea that anything so shocking as a murder had happened until I saw the notice in the street this morning. When I got into work a colleague, knowing that I always arrive via Griswell Road, showed me the piece in the Herald.

"That's when I knew I had to inform the police and I ran back to speak to your constable. I understand now that the poor man was shot, although I certainly didn't hear any gunfire. Her voice, measured and calm, now registered a note of unhappy concern. "Please tell me, Mr Bryce; if I'd stopped and attended to him, would he have survived?"

"I can safely say that you couldn't have saved him, Doctor. He was in hospital within minutes and pronounced inoperable. Incidentally, nobody else realised there had been a shooting until the ambulance men arrived – so you're hardly alone in that. We assume a silenced pistol was used.

"Let's talk about the woman. You've obviously heard that she was the killer, and probably carried out the murder in the instant before she moved out to pass the victim. What did you notice about her?"

Dr Metcalfe needed no time to answer. "Very little, I'm afraid. The most striking thing was her hair, shoulder length and very blonde. She was wearing a loose dress with yellow on it – I couldn't say if it was patterned or floral – and a cardigan in a similar yellow. Admittedly, it's not cold at present, but looking back, I'd have thought something a bit thicker and less summery would have been called for.

"Not that I was thinking about that at the time. She was carrying a shopping bag, and for all I knew, she was just slipping a few doors down the road and wouldn't be out for long. I wouldn't like to hazard a guess at her age, except to say that she certainly wasn't old. Between thirty-five and forty-five, if I was pressed to give an opinion.

"Does any of that help in any way?"

Bryce thought for a moment. "What you've said agrees with other reports, although so far you seem to be the only person who was facing the woman at any time. Look, Doctor Metcalfe, I'm going to give you a very restricted bit of information.

"We have good reason to think that the woman you and other people saw was actually a man in a woman's dress and wig. That said, would you like to think again about what you witnessed?"

"Oh, good heavens!" came the doctor's astonished exclamation. "I just don't know." She ran through her memory again. "I suppose my eyes were on the murderer, if that's who it was, for not more than two or three seconds – not long enough to pick up any of the tell-tale signs of a man impersonating a woman.

"But now you've raised the issue, Chief Superintendent, I'd have to say the hair supports your theory of a wig. Thinking about it, I don't believe many females over the age of about twenty-five would have hair like that – and I doubt many under that age, at least not in Stepney. It really was glamorous. But with that level of glamour comes a lot of expense, and a lot of time needed for maintenance.

"Time and money are not things the local women I see in my surgery have a lot of. They marry young and have several children quickly, and mostly live in horribly inadequate and overcrowded conditions.

"As for seeing a man in drag on the streets of London, one simply doesn't expect it. Perhaps in Soho at night, but not in broad daylight in the East End. No, it would never have occurred to me that was what I was seeing."

"All right, Doctor, thank you very much." There was nothing helpful in the GP's evidence but Bryce successfully kept his disappointment out of his voice. "Please don't mention the man/woman aspect to anybody at all; I'm trying to keep that within the Met at present."

"Will you want me to make a statement?"

"That won't be necessary for now, thank

you, and probably not at all. If we get a suspect, and hold an identity parade with a number of other men in similar wigs, we may ask you to come along and see if you can pick him out. Would you pass the telephone back to PC Rodway, please."

Bryce thanked the officer and instructed him to stand beside the board again the following morning. "Change the wording from 'yesterday' to 'Monday'. After tomorrow, you can give up."

Bryce put his feet up on his desk and leaned back in his chair as far as he could. He was aware of this habit, and tried to think when it had started, and what had initially triggered it. "I'm sure I never did this a year ago," he muttered to himself. He thought it must have coincided with his promotion – perhaps all senior officers did this automatically, almost subconsciously.

He realised the absurdity of this hypothesis the moment he thought it. The idea of the very staid Commissioner, or even one of the Assistant Commissioners, putting their feet up on a desk was too ludicrous to contemplate. However, he left his feet where they were.

Five minutes later, he was speaking to the friendly scientist at Hendon, who reported that all four bullets submitted had undoubtedly been fired from the same gun. A written report would be despatched within a couple of days.

The DCS rang down to Lomax. "You two carry on with your Allen investigations for the rest of the day, Sergeant. Come up to my office at half past eight in the morning, and we'll map out our next moves."

Bryce spent the remaining hour in discussions with DCI Nunn about various departmental matters, and dictating letters and memoranda to his Secretary.

Shortly before he was ready to leave off for the day, his telephone rang once more. George Fraser, a strong element of excitement in his voice, had good news.

"We're getting somewhere, Philip! I've cracked Robert Rennie. What he says boils down to this: McLeish was an important collector for one of Morton-Hugh's protection rackets, and was skimming the takings in a really greedy manner. Rennie didn't know the exact amount, but he reckoned perhaps five thousand in total. That was on top of what he was allowed to keep for himself, which was allegedly very generous indeed, and allowed McLeish to be quite the peacock during the war. Obviously, what he did couldn't be allowed; an example had to be made. The Weasel thinks McLeish got wind that he was due for a kneecapping or worse, and made off, taking his ill-gotten with him.

"Morton-Hugh was livid. Bad enough he's being hugely cheated; but if McLeish escapes, he's lost his grip on him. He's a loose cannon then. He could start selling all Morton-Hugh's secrets that he knows about. That would leave the man wide open to a takeover of his interests, never mind blackmail. That's when he tells Rennie to hunt McLeish down without worrying about cost.

"Rennie put his feelers out and found a gang leader in London – I'll tell you about him in a minute – who said his men had located McLeish and offered a thorough beating for two hundred pounds. Rennie reported to Morton-Hugh who allegedly said 'Not good enough. I want him finished once and for all'. Your London felon apparently promised a third party could be arranged for that job; total price of twelve hundred pounds, all payable in advance."

Bryce, thoroughly absorbed in the detail Fraser was giving him, put a question. "I don't understand how Rennie managed to identify McLeish to the complete strangers searching for him in London – and presumably elsewhere?"

The Scottish Superintendent sounded exasperated. "Aye, how indeed! We'd long suspected that one of Morton-Hugh's businesses was a photography studio, and that apart from the usual portraits and wedding pictures, there's an illegal pornography racket on the side.

"What we didn't know until Rennie exposed it all, is that Morton-Hugh arranges for a photograph of all his wee helpers – and their families if they have them – every two years or so. It's conditional – no photograph, no work. Let me tell you, Philip, it's blown wide open for us why his crew are so loyal to him. We couldnae understand his hold before, but now it's been laid bare for us."

Bryce was not easily shocked, but the idea that Morton-Hugh would keep his minions in never-ending servitude and silence by leaving a threat hanging over their families, was beyond repugnant to the DCS. "They're terrified and think there's no hiding place if they want to break away, much less run?"

"Aye. And you can be sure he let it be known that's how McLeish was tracked down. All Rennie had to do was release multiple prints of the latest photograph until someone came back to him shouting 'Bingo!' "

Fraser continued explaining how the arrangements were finalised. "With the go-ahead from Morton-Hugh, Rennie agrees the terms over the telephone. It's arranged the money will be paid in the usual way – old notes in a brown paper package. The Weasel himself will be the courier.

"He takes a train to Crewe to rendezvous with the London man coming up from Euston. They meet in the station bar on Tuesday 16th October, '45, and the cash is handed over. The London contact promises Rennie that the job will be done within a week. Which it was – four days later, actually.

"What do you think, Philip?"

"I think you've done wonders, George! Of course, your man Rennie has more or less pleaded to a charge of being an accessory before the fact, and unless he succeeds with the King's Evidence ploy he'll likely hang."

"Aye. Well, I promised him nothing – how could I? Not my decision. He's made a lengthy and very damning statement for us, but if I can only have the one, I'd still prefer Morton-Hugh to be on the trap over Rennie. We'd all rest more easily up here if we could send him to hell.

"Now for your London man who collected the money, Philip. Name of Trevor Walsh. D'you know him?"

"I know *of* him, certainly, but our paths have never crossed. The usual story – fingers in lots of pies, none of them legal. Very few convictions, though, as far as I remember.

"I'll crack on with everything you've given me, George, and let you know how it all pans out at this end. In the meantime, you've done me more than proud and I definitely owe you a bottle of single malt!"

CHAPTER 11

The next morning, Bryce arrived at his desk before his Secretary even entered the building – a very rare occurrence. Although he often worked late, he seldom 'burned the candle at both ends', recognising that time away from the job was a necessary condition of working effectively. He occupied himself clearing more paperwork, and when Mrs Pickford appeared asked her to have three cups of coffee ready for eight-thirty.

As expected, Lomax and Firth arrived at the same time as the refreshments. Bryce was soon giving his colleagues Doctor Metcalfe's scant recollections and observing two disappointed faces, both of which immediately brightened when he shared the news from Scotland.

"What have you two got?"

Lomax indicated that Firth should speak first.

"We took an Allen each, sir. I looked at Zachary or 'Zak' Allen. He's thirty-six. Several convictions pre-war, minor assaults mostly. Went into the army in 1940 and saw service overseas.

Our military liaison people checked him out and say his army record was okay – nothing adverse known, but still never managed to gain even a single stripe.

"He was a competent shot with a rifle – small bore and .303 – and trained to handle a Bren gun. No convictions since he was discharged. He used to live in Wapping, but two or three years ago moved out to Seven Kings, a decent area. Owns his own house and no mortgage. I can't find that he has a regular job."

"Sounds hopeful," said Bryce. "What about your man, Sergeant?"

"Nothing like as promising. Michael Allen, now thirty-eight. Also had convictions pre-war, some for dishonesty, a couple for common assault. He was rejected for war service on medical grounds but carried on being a nuisance in civvy street. Convicted again in '41 and '43, the last one getting him a twelve-month stretch for making off without payment.

"No suggestion that he's ever handled a gun of any sort. He's lived in the same house in Deptford since 1943. Allegedly picks up odd jobs for various people, making deliveries, that sort of thing. Probably all illegal. It's thought he's a part-time bookie's runner for a start. No sign of ever having money, sir."

"All right. If the Allen we want is one of these two, then Zak seems to be by far the more likely. It's time we talked to some of these people.

Let's try our erstwhile burglar, Sam Palmer, first. You two take a car, find him and invite him to accompany you to Leman Street. He used to live in Hornchurch, but may have moved. You'll have to get an address from Records.

"When you've got him, don't explain what this is about. Flash your warrant cards quickly and don't mention me or the Yard. Let him think this is about burglaries. If he demurs, you can arrest him on a charge of suspicion of conspiracy to murder and take him in anyway. But I'd much rather he arrives ignorant of what's going on. Give me a call when you've found him.

"Once he's safely in the station, I want you to find Trevor Walsh. He's the one who allegedly set the whole thing up. Get his address from Records while you're down there."

Bryce was uncomfortably aware that there was no evidence whatsoever to link Palmer with the second murder, other than the fact that Farncombe worked to fence goods stolen by his associates, together with a sketchy theoretical motive. Interviewing Palmer was also something of a risk. If he couldn't be detained after the interview, he might warn the killer as soon as he was released. Nevertheless, he calculated that the potential benefits outweighed the risks and was prepared to proceed on that basis.

With everything underway, he settled down to a morning of routine work, almost uninterrupted and making good progress until

Sergeant Lomax called at twenty past eleven.

"Found Palmer at home, sir. Came voluntarily, cool as a cucumber; made no objection at all. He's leaning on the front desk now, chatting to the Leman Street Custody Officer like they're old chums. Do you want him in a cell, or shall we put him in an interview room?"

"If everyone's happy with him in the reception area he can stay there and carry on thinking he's there for something and nothing." Bryce checked his watch. "I'll be with you in twenty to thirty minutes. Get him a brew and apologise. Tell him the officer who wants to talk to him has been delayed."

Bryce weighed up whether he should travel by underground or take his police car. Deciding that the traffic wouldn't be too bad at this time, he opted to drive, and parked in Leman Street within his estimate. He found Lomax and Field talking to the desk man, but no Sam Palmer.

"He's in interview room two, sir. He got tired of standing." reported Lomax.

The desk officer, who was relieving Sergeant Sawyer, suppressed a titter. Blowing out his cheeks he made a circle around his stomach with his arms and said, "He's a big boy and heavy on his feet, right enough!"

"I'll go and talk to him," said Bryce, "but before I do, whereabouts does Walsh live?"

"Barking, sir."

"Go and pick him up now, if you can find

him. Different tactics in his case. Arrest him straight away on suspicion of murder, but don't give him any clue which. Put him in cuffs. Mention me, but other than that, get him here in silence. All clear?"

Grins and nods told Bryce his orders, and the reasoning behind them, were understood. He made his way along the corridor to find Palmer leaning back in a chair with a mug in his hand.

"Hello, Sam. Remember me?"

Palmer had shown no sign of recognition as the Chief Superintendent entered the room, but now appeared to be retrieving a memory as the senior Yard detective took his seat. A light went on behind his eyes.

"Why yes, Mr Bryce, your posh voice just reminded me. You was a DI here five or six years ago. You tried to get me for a job I didn't do."

"Pull the other one, Sam. You were as guilty as they come, and the fact that I couldn't make the charge stick doesn't make you innocent – it just makes you lucky. But I'm not here to reminisce about the good old days. I'm a chief superintendent at the Yard now, and frankly I'm not interested in your burglary business."

Bryce held up a warning hand as Palmer appeared to be about to expostulate and protest his innocence of any involvement in burglary.

"I've got no time for fairy stories, Sam. Let's talk instead about more interesting things. Joseph Farncombe, for example."

As he spoke the name, the DCS was sure a sudden flash of fear crossed Palmer's face, but he recovered instantly.

"Name sort o' rings a bell."

"About as loud as the Great Bell of Bow used to be, I think. Your friends have used him as a fence for years. On your recommendation, if not directly on your behalf."

"No, no, Mr Bryce! Why should a someone like me be connected to a fence?"

Bryce let his annoyance be heard in his voice. "I've already told you, Sam, I don't want to listen to it. Tell me everything about Farncombe. Now."

Palmer hesitated. "I think I may have heard of him, rather than *know* him," he admitted, almost dragging the words out of himself.

Bryce slammed a hand down on the table. "That's the last time you're going to prevaricate, Sam. You're a thief through and through and have many disreputable acquaintances. We both know it, so stop pretending. Would you call Farncombe a friend?"

Palmer didn't look happy. "I wouldn't say he was a friend, exactly. More like someone I saw from time to time, is all."

"Did he do something to upset you?"

A blank look and a non-committal "Don't remember no falling out with him, Mr Bryce. In fact, I'm quite sure we parted on friendly terms, last time we met."

The lift of the Chief Superintendent's eyebrow told Palmer that he had overplayed his hand. He tried to back-pedal. "Not that I can even remember the last time we met – or what we chatted about."

"All right. Here's a nice big prod for your memory. We'll be talking to all of your gang while we've got you in here. Won't take us long to find everything out. My advice to you is cough it all up before they do.

"And while you're marshalling your memories, Sam, I'll tell you what I believe. My guess is you were worried because word got around that Farncombe was a grass. You were scared he knew enough about you to be worth a pony or two if he went to the Old Bill. Not to mention the fact that he was fed up with you constantly squeezing him for a bigger cut for yourself."

"Joe a grass? I'm shocked, Mr Bryce. I'd never have thought it of him in a million years." Palmer was doing his best to sound convincing.

"Well, the evidence is piling up against you. I'm just debating whether to charge you with murder, or whether to go easy on you and think of a non-capital offence. It's up to you, in a way. What do you suggest?"

Palmer said nothing, but the shudder that wobbled the flesh of his huge frame told Bryce that he was nervous. It was surprising he hadn't demanded a solicitor.

With no sign of a reply in the offing, Bryce set out his stall. "You make use of unpleasant people to, shall we say, persuade your enemies to toe the line. But I doubt if your regular henchmen would agree to go as far as murder for you. That needn't be a problem, though, because you're a well-connected man, and you must have heard of other ways to get rid of difficult individuals.

"Suppose you talk about that, Sam, hypothetically, of course. Oh, and don't bother telling me about some brassy blonde. We're fully aware that Farncombe's killer is male."

Once again, Palmer's face told a story. Eventually, and for the first time since he looked at the DCS when he entered the room, he met his eyes again.

"So the deal is, if I tell you how someone might get hold of a hitman, you won't charge me with murder?"

"No promises. Take your chances."

"All right. I don't want no murder rap 'cos I've never done no murder. I'll tell you something, but remember this is just general, what did you call it, hypothetical? I'd never do this myself."

"Understood."

"All I've ever heard, Mr Bryce, is that if you write a 'phone number on a bit of paper, put it in an envelope addressed to Mrs A, and leave it with the landlord of the Orb and Sceptre in Ilford, things might be arranged for you. At a price. They say you might need to cough up at least a bag of sand for a result. Old notes, not in sequence. All in advance."

Palmer passed pudgy fingers over his mouth. "Is that good enough for me?" It was almost a bleat.

Bryce looked at the fearful mound of a man opposite. "It may be, Sam. I freely admit that unless Mrs A claims you commissioned him to kill Farncombe, I'll find it very hard to prove that you did. For that reason, I'm not charging you at the moment. But I'm going to hold you here until tomorrow. I'm not having you sending a warning to Mrs A, care of the Orb and Sceptre."

"I'd not do that, Mr Bryce. If he knew I'd even given an 'int I'd be dead myself."

"Yes, I expect you would, Sam. Not that the world would have lost much." He stood up. "Come on. I'll have you transferred to a cell."

That exercise completed, Bryce considered whether to return to the Yard or wait at the station in the hope that his men would bring in Trevor Walsh quickly. He had brought his briefcase with him, with enough paperwork to last a while, and decided to take up residence again in the office he'd been given on Monday.

At half past one, he returned to his little café, ate a sustaining lunch, and then walked back down Leman Street to the police station.

At the front desk he found a middle-aged uniformed officer talking to the Desk Sergeant.

"This is Constable Paine, sir – I understand you wanted to speak to him."

"Yes, I do. Hello, Paine, I don't think this will take more than a couple of minutes so we'll stay here. Do stand easy. I'm Chief Superintendent Bryce, looking into the Griswell Road murder on Monday. But I'm also interested in that business at the Rabid Dog back in 1945. You were the first police officer on the scene, I understand. Cast your mind back. Describe for me what you found."

Paine was clearly not the brightest officer in the Met. He appeared to be struggling to assemble his thoughts, and this process took some thirty seconds. Eventually, he spoke.

"We had a call from some bloke, sir. Never found out who it was, but he said there was a dead man in the Dog. So I was sent to look. Horrible place, just the one bar. All pulled down now.

"Usually it was packed, but that night it wasn't even half full. Well, there was this man lying face up on the floor by the bar. Two ambulance men were there, and they said he was dead. I could see that for myself. They said they'd turned him over and seen a wound in his back, but then they'd put him back how they'd found him. I thought he might have been stabbed, so I told everyone to stay where they were. I started to ask if anyone knew who the man was, but nobody did. I was just feeling in his pockets for an ID card when Sergeant Blakely arrived, and Doctor Farrow with him.

"The doc said straight away that the man had been shot in the back, not stabbed.

"The Sarge sent me to a box to call the DDI. Took me some time to get hold of him, and he said he'd come at once. I went back to the Dog, but all I had to do was stand at the door and stop anyone coming in or out."

A classic example of the stable door, thought Bryce.

"When Mr Gilbert arrived, he took over. Soon after, he said the ambulance men could take the body away. The doc had already gone. I could see the DDI and the Sarge talking to the people in the bar, but I couldn't hear much of what was said. Soon after closing time, I was told I could leave. I made notes in my pocketbook, but I was never asked to make a statement.

"That's all I know, sir, except the case was all the talk in the station for months. Never solved, of course. I didn't work with the DDI, sir, but people said he got more and more down about it. The Sarge, he resigned soon after, and eventually Mr Gilbert retired."

Hardly surprising that PC Paine hadn't been asked to make a formal statement, thought Bryce. He basically had no evidence to give. It had been necessary to check with him now, but as it turned out it was a waste of time.

"All right, Paine, thank you. That's all; carry on."

***

The DCS retuned to his temporary office,

and started to work on the papers he had brought with him. By three o'clock he knew he would soon run out of paperwork and wondered if he'd made the right decision to wait. Two minutes later he had his answer, as Constable Firth arrived.

"Got Walsh, sir," he reported. "The Sarge is getting him booked in. Mr Walsh isn't a happy bunny and he's very jumpy."

"Well done. Have you two had anything to eat?"

"Yes, sir, we had to wait around for Walsh, so I got us some sandwiches to eat in the car before we picked him up."

"Okay. Go and ask someone to fix us up with three cups of tea, and then come back here with Sergeant Lomax. We'll let Walsh sit it out in the cells for a while."

Firth disappeared again. Ten minutes later, carrying a tray, he followed Lomax into the little office. There were sufficient chairs for the three men to sit, but precious little space between them. It was much the same size as the office Bryce had occupied in this building in 1946, although not the actual one. He looked around and appreciated how good his Yard accommodation was.

"Has Walsh said anything?" he enquired.

"Nothing significant, sir," replied Lomax. "He spluttered a bit when I told him he was under arrest. When we got him in the car, Firth gave him the line you told us to – that you were looking forward to seeing him on the gallows. He was very quiet after that. He hasn't asked for a solicitor."

The DCS gave his men a resumé of the interview with Palmer.

"Great stuff, sir!" exclaimed Firth. "What do you intend to do?"

"It's going to be a busy evening. When we've finished with Walsh – and I don't know how long that will go on – I want you to go to the Orb and Sceptre in Ilford. Arrest the landlord on suspicion of murder and bring him here. If there's another male barman use your discretion, but probably invite him to come along voluntarily too.

"You can both sit in on this next interview with your pocketbooks out. Extra bit of pressure, with three pairs of eyes on him and the two of you scribing."

"Palmer said 'Mrs A', so that suggests he's talking about Allen, doesn't it?" asked Firth.

"Yes, and Zak Allen lives in Barking, so very close to Ilford and this Orb and Sceptre place," added Lomax. He rubbed his hands together. "It's all looking good!"

Bryce nodded his agreement. "Yes, it all fits so far, but we're still very short of hard evidence to put in front of a jury. I've already told Palmer that we haven't got enough to prove he commissioned Farncombe's murder. This landlord will undoubtedly say he knew nothing of the purpose of the sealed messages, and it may be impossible to prove that he did. We'll see. If you've both finished your tea, let's go and talk to Walsh."

As they passed the front desk, the DCS asked the Sergeant to have Walsh brought out of the cells, and the three officers went to the cheerless little interview room. They didn't have long to wait.

Bryce had never seen Trevor Walsh either in real life or in a photograph, but the man now before him fitted the picture he had in his mind from hearing about him over a period of several years. He was aged about fifty, of medium height, with broad shoulders, short black hair flecked with grey, and a face that required two shaves a day. Normally, the DCS imagined, the facial expression would be hard – the sort needed to intimidate both underlings and dupes. The uniformed officer who brought him in removed his handcuffs on Bryce's instructions, and then withdrew.

"Caution him, please Sergeant."

The DCS was usually impeccably polite, sometimes even shaking hands with the suspect, and always using the title 'Mr' or 'Mrs' or any honorific as appropriate. Today, after Lomax had issued the formal caution, he broke with precedent.

"I won't say it's nice to meet you, Walsh, because I don't like to be in the same room with low-life such as you. But the job has to be done."

Walsh gave the detectives a sample of his usual braggadocio. "I've been misinformed, Mr Bryce. I've always heard you're a gent, but here you are being rude and arresting me on some stupid trumped-up charge. I may've done some bad-boy things in my day, but I've never killed nobody – and you know it."

Bryce sighed and tut-tutted. "You're not much of a mind reader, Walsh. I'll tell you what I know. I know that you're not even curious about which murder I've brought you in for." He looked towards his little team. "What should we make of that, I wonder?"

Lomax was first to offer a suggestion. "Oh, he knows exactly which one it is, sir. He's just not saying."

Firth gleefully jumped in with "I reckon he's up to his neck in so many he's lost count, and doesn't know which one you've nabbed him for."

Walsh's eyes widened to their fullest extent as he listened to the detectives' exchange.

The Chief Superintendent addressed him again. "I'm not suggesting that you personally killed anyone. No, no. Why would you, when you can always get others to do your dirty work? But you shouldn't let that make you feel happier. In case you don't know the particular point of law that I intend to rely on, I'll explain it for you: giving the order to kill someone will get you hanged just the same as if you did do that particularly vile crime yourself."

Walsh looked at the three implacable faces across the table. He did a slightly better job of concealing his feelings than had Palmer in the same room earlier, but all the detectives could see that he was worried.

"I've not given orders to kill no-one. Never."

"All right. Let's talk about something else. Me, I'm very interested in steam locomotives and railway systems. What about you?"

Walsh stared back at Bryce in total bemusement. "Eh?" was all he could manage in reply.

"Well, when I have some spare time, or on holiday, I go by train to various interesting places. I try to observe vintage locomotives, look at the station architecture, and so on. What about you?"

With no idea of where this conversational gambit was going, but feeling confident enough to laugh and answer, Walsh said, "I'm a Londoner, born and bred. Like a lot of men, I just missed the first war and was too old for the last.

"Result is, I've never been nowhere and never felt the need to go anywhere. Even stay in London if I get the odd day's holiday. Course, I use the tube like anyone else. That's it." With an injection of sarcasm he added, "I don't feel safe outside our well-policed Metropolitan area, Mr Bryce."

"I see. I was just wondering why you once took a train to Crewe. A very important railway town, but not the sort of place one goes to for a day trip from London. Especially if the duration of your excursion was so short that you couldn't spare time to take even one step outside the station. No doubt you can explain?"

The observers could almost see Walsh's brain attempting to process this unwelcome question. Unwisely, he chose to deny the visit.

For the second time he said "Don't know what you mean. I've hardly 'eard of this place, and I've never been to it. Honest."

"You shouldn't use words you don't understand. You haven't been honest since you were a babe in arms.

"Happily, I'm in a position to augment your sadly failing memory. On October the 16th, 1945, you took a train from Euston. You got out at Crewe and went into the station refreshment rooms. There you met your Glaswegian equivalent, a Scottish felon named Robert Rennie, who works for Andrew Morton-Hugh. Rennie handed you an envelope containing twelve hundred pounds. You took the next train back to the smoke. Ring any bells so far?"

Walsh sat and said nothing, but his Adam's apple bobbed as he swallowed.

"Then, and you'll say this is just a coincidence, three days later a murder was committed in a low public house by the docks."

"Course it was coincidence. These things 'appen."

"Yes, unfortunately they do. But it also happens that the victim in this particular case was a man whom Rennie's boss desperately wanted to eliminate. When you appear at the Old Bailey

I wonder if your jury will believe in that being coincidence? Not to mention the fact that the money paid to you by Rennie just happens to be the fee charged by a certain assassin – plus your fee for arranging it, of course.

"And when they hear Rennie's testimony about the earlier conversations between the two of you, I think they'll have no doubt as to your guilt."

Walsh was looking quite grey. "I want my solicitor."

"Of course you do. But first, one other point. When your solicitor arrives, I shall charge you with murder, with an alternative charge of being an accessory before the fact. Both carry the same penalty. After I've done that, there can be no going back.

"If you prefer, I'm willing to let you talk just a little more now. Specifically, you might like to tell us all about 'Mrs A'. We'll put you back in the cells for fifteen minutes to think about it. At the end of that time, you'll have to decide which way you're going to jump – into the long arms of the law, or at the end of a rope. Your choice.

"Escort him back to the Custody Officer, please Constable."

Firth returned within a minute. "Walsh is nearly wetting himself, sir. But is a conviction as certain as you implied?"

"Unfortunately, no, it isn't. The more interviews you observe the more you'll appreciate how much brinksmanship and finessing is involved. As a witness, a man like Rennie with numerous previous convictions himself could be portrayed by the defence as unreliable in the extreme.

"But attacking the antecedents of a prosecution witness also carries risk for a defendant like Walsh, who has previous matters he'd prefer to keep from the jury. The fact remains, however, that if Walsh sticks to his story and says he never went to Crewe we only have one dodgy witness who says he did.

"Even so, I'd certainly like that denial in writing from him if it's all I can get on the matter. Beyond that, I hope to find some tangible connection between Walsh and 'Mrs A'. If we could even show that they knew each other it would help."

"Will you allow him to turn King's Evidence, sir?" asked Lomax.

"That's not for me to say, Sergeant. Treasury Counsel, probably in consultation with the Attorney General, makes that sort of decision. But this may be a case where some sort of deal could be done. Whatever happens, though, I don't see Walsh walking the streets of London for the next fifteen years."

The three detectives talked about how best to make the arrest at the Orb and Sceptre, until Bryce decided Walsh had had long enough. "Get him brought back, please," he instructed Firth.

"What do you want to do?" asked Bryce

peremptorily, almost before his prisoner had sat down.

"What're you offerin' me?" Composure had returned to Walsh's manner.

"Nothing. Nothing at all. If you tell us something that at least looks promising, you can talk it all over with your solicitor and I'll put off charging you until tomorrow. Then, depending how accurate and useful your information turns out to be, I might recommend a lesser charge to the powers that be. Take it or leave it, it's the best you'll get."

Walsh prefixed his next remark with some ugly curse words. "That Rennie, no wonder they call him the Weasel. I don't fancy 'is chances of reaching old age when the 'big yin' finds out he squealed."

"He'll likely have a better chance than his boss, who'll definitely be taking the eight o'clock walk," commented Bryce. "But go on."

"You reckon it's my choice, but you know as well as I do it's not, cos there isn't a choice!" Walsh spat out bitterly, before he gave up the necessary details.

What he said concurred exactly with Sam Palmer's story earlier. He identified the public house as the contact point, the messages to 'Mrs A', and the fee payable for a hit. He then came to a halt and looked hopefully at the DCS.

"You can do a bit better than that, and you'll need to if you want the chance of leniency. Let's have the name. And no baloney about Mrs A being a woman."

Walsh, surprised again, put his head in his hands and groaned. "God help me, and I just hope you pick him up before he finds out I'm in here. It's Zachary Allen."

"At least we know you're telling the truth now. Do you meet him yourself?"

"No. I knew him years ago, before the war. But for the last few years he keeps completely out of sight. I don't even know where he lives now. Messages go through the Orb. An' I'm pretty sure he don't ever go in there hisself. There'll be a messenger, and then prob'ly a cut-out."

"Who else would know about him?"

"Enough would know about 'Mrs A'. Not many'd know how to contact 'im. 'Arf a dozen of the top crime men, maybe. That's 'ow 'e gets 'is jobs, through the likes of us. 'Is real name, though, well maybe not even as many as six that'd likely know it."

"What about Joseph Farncombe? Would he qualify as a 'top crime man'?"

"I reckon. He was the best fence in London on account of never bein' caught over a good few years. I know him and Sam Palmer was close, and Sam knew Allen, for sure. But then word went round that Joe had grassed someone up. That'll be why he got put out."

Bryce nodded, satisfied that he'd heard enough. "All right. Take him back again, Constable.

Tell the Custody Sergeant I'm holding him overnight without charge, and ask him to call whichever solicitor he wants."

When Firth returned, Bryce looked at the two officers. "Do you feel like doing the pub arrest tonight?"

The junior men exchanged a glance. "We're all set to go, sir," said the Sergeant.

"Thanks. I want to get back to my own office now, so assuming you can get the landlord, arrest him and bring him straight to the Yard, not here. Suspicion of being an accessory to murder should do to hold him.

"Before you call at the pub, drop into Ilford police station. Find out the name of the landlord of the Orb and Sceptre before you pick him up. At the same time, let the Ilford boys know you're making an arrest on their patch."

CHAPTER 12

On reaching his desk, Bryce immediately began to draft an 'information' to justify his application for a warrant to enter Zachary Allen's property. It was nearly five o'clock when he completed this task, and he telephoned the nearest courthouse to see if a magistrate would be available. The answer was in the affirmative, so he set off on foot to make the five-minute journey.

He saw the stipendiary in his room and needed only a few minutes to convince him that a warrant was necessary. Half an hour after he left his office, Bryce was back, arriving just in time to say good night to Mrs Pickford as she was covering her typewriter before going home.

He called Jack Nunn to say he had returned, and learned that several other newspapers – "probably every national daily and Sunday paper" – had been on the telephone during the day. He wondered what they would find to tell their readers. Those papers with investigation departments would no doubt have more reporters like Jeremy Grieves sniffing around, and it was surprising that he hadn't seen any around Leman Street. He hoped that nothing would be done to alert Allen. It was a risk leaving the raid on Allen's house for another day, but Bryce always preferred to build up a case as much as possible rather than rush precipitately into making an arrest which might not stick.

Next, he called Mile End Hospital, something he felt he should have done before. Asking for Staff Nurse Donaldson, he was put through to the Sister's office on that ward. Here he was in luck, because Staff Nurse Donaldson was not only on duty, but was available to be brought to the telephone.

Bryce introduced himself, and thanked the nurse for her statement. "I hope you haven't been plagued by reporters and the like?"

"No, not at all, Chief Superintendent. I understand some have come to the hospital, trying to learn more about Mr Farncombe. But they haven't found out much, and fortunately they don't know about me anyway. Sister told me that Matron spoke to some of the consultants, and it was decided to deploy a few porters to remove unauthorised visitors from the site. So I'm fine, thank you. May I ask if you're getting anywhere?"

"Oh yes. For your ears only, Miss Donaldson, I hope to arrest someone tomorrow. I'll let you know if everything goes according to plan."

After this conversation, Bryce spent a useful twenty minutes on paperwork, before the Desk

Sergeant called to say that DS Lomax had brought a man into custody.

"Good. Lock him up, please, and send Lomax and Firth up here. I'll come and sort out your paperwork shortly."

"Who have you got, then?" enquired Bryce five minutes later when his detectives had joined him.

"Nathan Scott, sir, the licensee. We checked, by the way, and he has a clean record. It was quite funny, really. It was almost opening time, and the landlord himself unlocked the door when we knocked. He was the only person there – his wife left him years ago with a regular, he said. So we arrested him, locked the door again, and came away."

Firth laughed. "Wish every arrest was as neat!"

Lomax agreed and continued to describe events for Bryce. "Doubt if anyone saw us, either, because there was nobody in the street as we came out. Scott told us in the car that his chief barmaid has a key, so no doubt she'll open the pub as usual, but she and a lot of other people will be wondering where he's gone!"

Bryce smiled. "A bit of mystery for them to dwell on won't hurt. Let's go and see him. I'm not expecting any great revelations, but it'll be interesting to hear his explanation."

Scott was brought into an interview room, and sat down opposite the three officers. The

Chief Superintendent introduced himself to the weedy-looking Londoner, who appeared closer to seventy than sixty. Very sparse white hair topped a wrinkled face, with blood-shot blue eyes behind spectacles which had so much tape holding them together the frame was hardly visible.

The publican opened up the conversation aggressively. "You can't pin nothing on me, I'm clean!" he snarled in an unexpectedly deep voice.

"You're very far from clean, Mr Scott. For years you've allowed criminals to use your pub as a recruiting bureau for a murderer. We've already amassed a great deal of evidence, so don't try to pretend you didn't know anything about it."

"I don't need to pretend! I don't run no sort of bureau from my pub. If you mean people leave messages for other people, then yeah, lots of 'em do. I don't read the messages or even enquire what's in 'em – none of my business. It's not illegal to provide a message forwarding service!"

"I see." Bryce uncapped his fountain pen and positioned the nib over the foolscap pad before him. "Give me all the names of the other people who leave messages with you, and to whom they're addressed."

Scott was silent.

"No? Very well, let's talk about the messages addressed to 'Mrs A'. I certainly believe you when you say you've never enquired what was in them. You wouldn't be so foolish as to do that.

"Talk me through the procedure when one

arrives, because 'Mrs A' doesn't come in every day to see if anyone has left her a communication. So how do the messages get to her?"

Scott was weighing up how much he needed to reveal to clear himself with the police, against how much he would need to withhold in order to keep himself safe from attack when he left the station. He offered the bare minimum. "A boy comes in and takes them."

"Good. I'll accept that. Same boy every time?"

"No. I don't remember seein' the same one twice."

"I'm prepared to believe that's also true, because these messages wouldn't be very frequent. But there again, don't try telling me a different boy comes in every day, or even once a week, on the off chance that there might be a message waiting."

The landlord sat silently again.

Bryce's tone became affable. "You've done unusually well compared with all the other liars we've seen in here, Nathan. We've had a couple of truthful answers on the trot from you. Let's see if you can't make it a hat trick with my next question." He crossed his arms and leaned forward on the small table, his eyes never leaving publican's face. "The only way the system could work is if you take the initiative and ensure that Mrs A knows there is a message. Am I right?"

Scott had instinctively moved back as the DCS moved forwards, his eyes darting around from detective to detective, but he didn't answer. He was again calculating what he could safely say when Bryce forestalled him by laying bare the crux of the deception.

"Perhaps I should tell you that we already know who 'Mrs A' is – or rather, who Mr A is. And I'll also tell you I'm prepared to believe that you don't call him direct. Not because I've suddenly decided you're a truthful person, but because we've already been told that Mr A uses a cut-out.

"We'd like to talk to that cut-out, Nathan. Why not tell us who it is that you make arrangements with, to pass on the fact that a message is waiting?"

Scott started to shake. He looked imploringly at the faces opposite. "You know I can't grass. I'd be as good as dead!"

Bryce assumed a perplexed tone. "But Nathan, you've been aiding and abetting a murderer. That doesn't result in longevity, you know, because we could call you an accessory before the fact." He now bore down on Scott's worst fear. "And the penalty for being an accessory before the fact is the same as Mr A will get."

The landlord retreated into silence again.

Bryce allowed him a short respite from questioning before giving him some information, and delivering what he hoped would be the final push Scott needed to offer up everything he knew. "You really don't need to worry about 'Mr A'. We'll have him in custody very soon and on the end of a rope shortly after that. But right now, we'd like you to co-operate with our enquiries.

"Of course, you're at liberty to choose not to co-operate, Nathan, but then we'll be obliged to bear in mind those charges I just mentioned. After which, there can't be any liberty for you."

Astonishingly, Scott still held out.

Bryce, knowing that it was momentum in interviews which most successfully produced results, was unwilling to allow a prolonged silence. He played the last and weakest card in his hand but did so as if he was delivering the mortal blow.

"No comment, Nathan?"

He abruptly stood up. Lomax and Firth instantly followed suit, the latter shoving his chair under the table in a particularly decisive manner, and with a self-satisfied 'we've got you now' expression, fully believing that the DCS had a winning ace to deliver.

"We'll be getting your telephone records from the GPO next," said Bryce. "Then we can see who you've called besides the brewery and the Licensed Victuallers Association. It would have been far better for you if we didn't have to go to the bother, because then we could have said that you'd been helpful. As it is…"

Scott was almost in tears as he snivelled out his response. "I'd die in stir, guv – I'm not goin' there! I'll give you what you want, but you 'ave to keep me out of prison. You 'ave to!"

He wiped his nose on the back of his hand.

"As God's me witness I don't know who Mr A is an' I swear I never even knew he was a mister. If I thought anything – 'an I never did – it was that Mrs A would be another go between. His mum or his missus.

"I never set eyes on 'im or 'er or whoever. Just the boys that brung the notes. Never seen the cut-out neither. All I do is ring him. Bloke called Billy. Number is GOO 903. That's it. That's all I've ever known."

Bryce brought his hands together in one loud clap. "Well done, Nathan! That wasn't so bad, was it? We'll treat you to bed and board here tonight and think about what to do with you in the morning."

The landlord looked as though 'that' was as bad as it could possibly have been from his point of view, but said nothing as Firth escorted him out.

Returning minutes later, the Constable found his superiors were again seated. "The number he gave is on the Goodmayes exchange, sir, right next door to Seven Kings."

Firth almost didn't raise the doubt in his mind, but then remembered Lomax's previous advice, and the encouragement he had so far been given. "What you said about tracing his calls, sir, could you really do that?"

A rueful, "Not any more," was Bryce's response. "Or at least, not if Scott's exchange has been automated – and there aren't many manual ones left now. A bluff on my part, I'm afraid, but I'm glad it paid off. Either he wasn't thinking straight, or he doesn't understand the GPO telephone system.

"We'll have a talk with this character who goes by the name of Billy, tomorrow. It would be good news for us if he's the direct link to Allen, but it's possible there's yet another cut-out.

"As for tomorrow morning, gentlemen, we need an early start. Be here, ready to go, at six thirty. At other times of the year we'd be going in earlier, but we need adequate daylight for an armed raid. I have a search warrant, although if Allen is there and we arrest him we can go in anyway."

Bryce delivered the warning he always gave to officers who hadn't undergone firearms training. "Bear in mind that we're moving in on a man who not only has a pistol, but has already used it to kill. The old adage 'might as well be hanged for a sheep as for a lamb' is a very pertinent one when rounding up a homicide suspect, in a situation where he may well shoot his way out of a trap.

"Some of us will be armed – no question about that. As neither of you is qualified to carry weapons, I've drafted in three uniformed officers who are. Inspector Davey and I will go in from the front, and Sergeants Brooker and Prentice from the rear. You'll come with me, Firth, and you'll go with your fellow sergeants, Lomax.

"If there is any shooting, or even if Allen

appears holding a gun, you both take cover. Get right down. Whatever happens don't try to tackle him – leave that to those of us who are armed.

"That's it for today, gentlemen. Go home both of you, and get a good rest."

***

Bryce gave his wife a summary of the day's events. Given the risks involved in the morning, and not wanting to worry her, he didn't mention the planned raid.

However, when he rose very early the next morning, Veronica was instantly wide awake and immediately worked out what was to happen.

"Please take great care, Philip; I really don't know what Fleur and I would do without you." She didn't add, but thought to herself, 'I've already lost one husband and don't want to to lose another.'

"It'll be fine, Vee." He tried an old joke to lift her spirits and lighten her sombre expression. "I went through the war being shot at, and I wasn't killed even once!"

"Yes, but I didn't know you then. And there's the saying about nine lives." Veronica's head turned towards their open bedroom door. Fleur was announcing her need for her morning feed. "Just be very careful, for both of us as well as yourself, darling."

CHAPTER 13

A few minutes before six-thirty, the team of detectives and armed uniformed men was assembled in Bryce's office. He spent ten minutes briefing them and covering various possible scenarios.

"One last thing for those of you who are armed. If Allen fires any shots, or even points a gun at you, shoot to kill."

The six men left the Yard in two cars. Traffic was light, and it took only twenty-five minutes to reach Seven Kings. Adhering to the prior arrangement, the car with the three sergeants went to the road at the rear of the property.

It was unfortunate that Allen happened to be standing at the dressing table in front of his bedroom window, combing his hair after getting dressed. He saw the three officers – two in uniform entering his back garden. He also saw that two of them were carrying automatic pistols.

Within seconds he had snatched up his own pistol, kept in his bedside cupboard without the silencer in place, and was flying down the stairs.

He pulled open the front door and dashed down the three steps into the front garden. Facing him not thirty feet away were three more men. Bryce and Davey brought up their pistols, but Allen fired twice. One shot struck Inspector Davey, who fell to the ground. Firth was a couple of paces behind the two more senior officers, but the second shot passed through the gap between them and hit him. He stopped in shock.

Within half a second of the two shots, and before Allen's gun could move towards him, Bryce also fired twice. Shooting accurately from waist level with a handgun is not as easy as the cinema portrays, especially when both parties are on the move. The DCS intended to go for the heart, but in fact one of his shots hit his target in the left shoulder, and the other in the left upper arm. The pistol dropped from Allen's fingers, and he screamed in pain.

Bryce was onto him in a flash, kicking the gun out of reach, at the same time registering that it was a Colt, and not the Walther PPK he half-expected. He ignored the fact for the moment, and with his own automatic still covering the now prone man, he drew his whistle and gave a series of piercing blasts.

Local residents, looking from behind their curtains when they heard the gunfire, now nervously appeared from the neighbouring properties.

"Police!" Bryce bellowed at them. "Call for

two ambulances as quick as you can, then stay indoors!" He saw three men disappear back into their houses, hopefully one of whom had a telephone and could do as he had asked.

The second police car, driven by Lomax, now came roaring down the street. Bryce gave terse instructions to the two sergeants who emerged, realising that the missing Sergeant Brooker must still be covering the rear of the house.

"Prentice, you tend to Davey and Firth. Use the medical kits in both cars.

"Lomax, I've asked neighbours to call for ambulances but use the car wireless to make sure. I'll keep Allen covered until you're back."

Lomax returned within a minute. "All in hand, sir. Shall I 'cuff Allen now?"

"Yes; to the railings beside the steps. And search him thoroughly."

Allen, silent until now, started yelping loudly. In the process of emptying his pockets, Lomax was pulling him around far from gently, his every movement conveying his fury that two of his colleagues had been injured.

In next to no time, Allen's getaway goods were safely in evidence bags: two IDs, a box of bullets, and three thick rolls of banknotes. Lomax pocketed the bunch of keys he found.

The biggest surprise to the Sergeant was that Allen was also carrying small change. At first glance, this seemed unnecessary. It took him a moment to work out that Allen was, in fact, intelligently hedging his escape. If he could get to his vehicle and use his ignition key, that would be all well and good – probably ideal – from his point of view. But if his best escape was to run and then jump onto a passing bus, pulling out a roll of banknotes to pay a small fare would draw a great deal of unwanted attention to himself. The coins went into the bag with the banknotes.

With his prisoner tethered, Bryce slipped his safety catch on and walked back to his colleagues. He was greatly relieved to see that neither appeared badly hurt. Davey had been hit in the thigh, but the wound wasn't bleeding heavily, and the bullet had passed through cleanly without striking either bone or artery. Firth was similarly lucky, having taken another in-and-out shot, his in the upper arm. Both were more shocked than critically injured.

Only when he'd done his best for his colleagues did Prentice turn to the injured gunman, who was not as stoic as the men he had fired at – perhaps unsurprisingly, as one of Bryce's bullets had shattered the bone in his upper arm, and the other was lodged against his shoulder blade.

Bryce was commiserating with his wounded men when a pair of ambulances drew up, followed by two more police cars. These had been summoned by neighbours before it was realised that the police were already involved. Leaving his men, he went to meet the new officers and identified himself. Assured that everything was under control and that reinforcements were not needed, the two cars turned around.

To the four waiting ambulance men Bryce said, "We have three men with gunshot wounds. Where will you take them?"

"The King George in Ilford."

"Right, my two officers go first in one ambulance. The man over there by the railings goes in the other with his police escorts. He's going to be charged with murder. When you get to the hospital make sure my wounded men go in first and take priority over him."

The ambulance crews followed him to the front garden where Bryce squatted beside his colleagues. "I'm sending you together in one ambulance and I'll come and visit you as soon as I can. Would you like me to call anyone to let them know what's happened?"

Both officers, pale and shaken but bearing up well, turned down the offer.

"Thanks, sir, but you can't get hold of my wife," said Davey. "She's on her way to Penzance as we speak, to visit her sister. Time she gets there, I'll be able to call her myself."

Firth, having been placed with Barnardos when abandoned by his mother, had no relations to contact. Bryce made a mental note to ensure he was not left without visitors during his hospital stay. He waved forward both of the crews. "These men first."

Moving away to deal with Allen, Bryce heard one of the ambulance men jovially asking Firth, "You a walking wounded, mate, or would you prefer a little lie-down on a stretcher, like your pal with the hole in his leg?"

For a split-second, Bryce was back at Anzio, hearing again that encouraging lie 'we'll have you fixed up in no time, boy, good as new,' to even the most hopeless of cases. He looked back at the ambulance men. Two were gently lifting Davey into the back of the first vehicle. Firth, supported by the other pair, was standing on the pavement. Bryce didn't know which man had spoken to his DC, but briefly wondered if he had served with any of the four in those hellish war days. 'Were we men at arms together?' was a thought that would come back to him at unexpected times and in unexpected places, on the tube or bus, as he sat with complete strangers.

Sergeant Brooker was now running down the road towards them and Bryce's attention was once again back on his prisoner. "All right, Prentice, Brooker is about to join us, and the second ambulance crew will be back in a moment. You'll both escort Allen to hospital in their vehicle. Cuff him to yourself, Prentice, before unhooking him from the railings."

As soon as Brooker arrived, Bryce immediately sent the armed officer in through the front door to do a quick check. Once he returned with the confirmation that there was nobody else in the house, Bryce continued his orders to both men.

"When you get him to hospital, anchor him to his bed and stay with him. Everywhere he goes, you go. Under no circumstances is he to be left without one of you with him. Other than receiving medical attention his bracelets aren't to be removed for more than a minute and only then if absolutely necessary and with both of you present. I'll arrange for you to be relieved when I can find other officers."

The three policemen went back to the house steps where Lomax was watching Allen.

Hunkering down by the railings, Bryce looked at the assassin properly for the first time, remembering from police records that Allen was thirty-six. Despite the fact that his features were distorted with grimaces of pain, it was clear that he had a rounded, distinctly baby-shaped face compared with the typical, squarer jaw, of most men. He was also of a very slight build and no great height. As a result, he looked both younger than his years and also more effeminate. Trying to visualise him in a blonde wig, Bryce thought that even when seen from the front he might quite easily pass muster as a female with most people who weren't looking too closely, or for too long.

Addressing his captive he said, "Zachary Allen, you are under arrest on suspicion of murder. I'll be along to see you later."

The first ambulance was getting speedily

underway now, its bells jangling loudly, just as the second crew came up the path to fetch Allen. Bryce and Lomax were left in the front garden as Brooker and Prentice accompanied their prisoner to the hospital.

Lomax, retrieving his handcuffs from the railings, experienced a small burst of satisfaction that the second crew didn't bother to ring their bell – or drive at anything like the speed of the first ambulance. He held out Allen's keys to his boss. "All he had on him were these four, sir. One's definitely an ignition key. There's a garage round the back, detached from the house and accessed from the road behind."

The DCS accepted the keys. Picking up Allen's gun, which he noted was a Colt 1903, he made it safe, and dropped it into another evidence bag. Holding this and his own car keys out to Lomax, he said, "Take everything we've rounded up so far and lock it in my car boot. Bring back the murder bag."

"What a shambles," he muttered to himself as he reviewed the morning's events with dissatisfaction. When Lomax returned he remarked, "The way Allen came out of the door like a rabbit with a ferret behind it, I assume he must have seen you?"

"Unfortunately, yes. I noticed him looking out of an upstairs window. He saw us and disappeared in a flash. We heard the shots just as we reached the back door. That must be barred on the inside because there's no lock on the outside – and it's made of iron, as we soon found out. No breaching that without oxy-acetylene gear. The ground floor windows at the back are barred too. When we realised we couldn't get into the house, Brooker stayed to cover the back, and Prentice and I brought the car round to join the rest of you."

"He's obviously adapted the house to make himself as safe as possible," commented Bryce. "Almost certainly to protect himself from the enemies who might come after him. He could delay them until he'd called us for help. But no point in locking himself in when its the police confronting him; we could have cut off all his utilities and starved him out. His only hope was to escape by shooting his way out. One positive thing out of that mess was that it proved he's left-handed."

Lomax, quietly shocked at how quickly and violently events had unfolded, managed a thin smile. "Could be said we were trying to kill him too, sir, but legally via the gallows."

"That's true, I suppose. Right, let's look out the back first."

The two detectives walked through Allen's property and found the rear entrance. Bryce first examined the iron door. "No keyhole as you said, Sergeant; only operable from inside; interesting."

He removed the heavy bar securing the door and opened it, noticing how easily this was accomplished and also how slim the door was. Someone very skilful indeed had been commissioned to make not just the door, but also the iron frame and hinges – well-balanced and greased – which allowed the whole to move so smoothly and almost effortlessly on the part of anyone operating it.

One of the keys fitted the padlock on the garage doors, but even before Lomax got the first door open it was clear that no vehicle had gone in or out of the building for several years. Inside, they found a lawnmower and a few tools.

"No joy here," said Bryce, "and I can't say I'm surprised. A garage opening onto the road would be too easy to access for someone else who knew this was Allen's house.

"Lock up again, and we'll search inside. I doubt if we'll find any written evidence, but in the absence of discovering the green Singer in his garage, there are things I particularly do want from his house – the pistol he used with its silencer and the wig, above all else. Also, if there's no sign of a female occupant, any female clothing."

Back inside, both men noticed that the front door, still standing open, was also of the same exceptional construction as the back door, although painted to look like natural wood. The ground floor front windows were not barred like those at the rear, but were made of metal with small glazed panes. One of the keys on the bunch fitted the unusual front door lock.

"It's far better defended at the back,"

observed Lomax. "Probably less chance of a frontal attack with all the neighbours, so I suppose he felt he didn't need quite as much protection on this side."

"Yes. But has it occurred to you that it's as well he opened the door for us? Otherwise we'd have quickly found that we couldn't just jemmy it open or even shoot the lock off ourselves, and we'd have been in a siege situation. Although he couldn't have got away, it would have tied up lots of officers for days."

He thumbed towards the lounge. "You take a look in there first."

Bryce walked quickly around the rest of the house before starting to search himself. In the large back bedroom which Allen clearly used, he saw exactly what Lomax meant about the rear of the property. In fact, it was bad luck that Allen saw the policemen at all, because trees and shrubs obscured the view of the back roadway, as well as a good portion of the garden from the house. Also, he could see that any intruder wanting to get in wouldn't be visible from any other house once they were in the garden. Hence the extraordinary fortifications.

There was, unusually, an extension telephone in this bedroom. The DCS decided to make some essential calls before searching. He telephoned his wife first, to assure her that he was unharmed. He didn't mention the two wounded officers, thinking that would be better explained face-to-face.

Next, he called the Leman Street Superintendent.

"We have your man, Superintendent. Zachary Allen. I had to shoot him, but he's not fatally wounded. He's in the King George at Ilford. I've got two uniformed Yard men with him at present, but you'll need to provide a continuous two-man guard on him until he can be transferred to the prison hospital in the 'Ville. Can you set that up immediately?"

"Marvellous news, sir! I'll make the arrangements to relieve your men at once. Is he good for both killings?"

"I think so, yes. And maybe at least one more, but I still have some outstanding evidence to gather. I also have a few more people involved in his crimes dotted about in various cells. I'll come and brief you on everything later."

Bryce next called Mile End Hospital, as he had promised. He learned that neither Nurse Donaldson nor the Ward Sister were on duty until nine o'clock, and said he would call back later.

Lomax stuck his head into the bedroom as the DCS replaced the receiver. "Really nice place, this, sir, all furnished in a money-no-object sort of way. Two more bedrooms, but no sign of anyone else living here, and absolutely nothing female or the gun anywhere."

"We'll do this room together, then," said Bryce, "beginning with the bed."

The detectives thoroughly inspected every aspect of the mattress and bedding, but revealed no secret pockets or compartments where any of the items they were seeking could possibly be hidden. Lomax even unscrewed the brass finials on the bedstead, to see if anything had been stuffed into the hollow columns of the bedposts.

"You take a look in that wardrobe now, Sergeant, while I go through all the drawers."

Bryce immediately found a silencer – which appeared to be for the pistol Allen had just used against them. It was an accessory which the gunman obviously felt he needed to keep close to hand with his second gun. And what better place than in a bedside table, in case he should be surprised in the hours of darkness, when at his most vulnerable.

Lomax had pulled out the entire contents of the wardrobe and found nothing apart from men's clothing. He turned to his boss. "Would everything we've got from witnesses so far, without the gun, van, dress or wig be enough, sir? Because I don't believe there's anything else here."

Bryce looked doubtful. "Perhaps, if the Colt he used today proves to be the murder weapon. But bear in mind that until today no one has seen or heard Allen fire a single shot. Unlikely though it might be, experienced counsel might persuade a gullible jury to accept that Allen was merely storing the gun for someone else. The wig would cement the case for us. That and the relevant gun are the two things that tie Allen indisputably to our two murders. The dress, the cardigan, and the van are extras that we know about from Farncombe's murder, but none of those were mentioned in the Rabid Dog case."

He looked around the room again. "We absolutely need that key evidence, and I still think it's in the house somewhere. We keep looking."

Lomax was quite prepared to follow his Chief's lead, but nevertheless advanced an opinion which had gained more and more traction in his mind during their fruitless searching so far. "He might keep everything in the van, though, all locked up until he next needs it."

Bryce acknowledged this was a valid suggestion. "You make a good point, Sergeant. But we know from our line of work that lock-ups are constantly broken into, with the vehicles and everything in them stolen. Why would he take even the smallest risk of that happening – and with such publicised and incriminating evidence in it – when he's created such a fortress here? Doesn't make sense.

"No, we're going to pull this place apart if we have to, and we'll begin by checking for false backs or bottoms to the wardrobes and other furniture."

The detectives split up, but again, this new approach produced nothing. Neither did an inspection of the loft. Lomax, being the taller of the two, first used a chair to reach up and push aside the hatch cover, and then the Chief Super's shoulders to clamber up and search.

Fed up and weary, the detectives took a break in Allen's lounge. All the furniture here had been upended by Lomax to see if anything was taped to the bottom or concealed in any other way. The chimney flue in this room (like the others in the house) had been explored with a poker bringing down nothing but soot. A floor-standing potted parlour palm had been uprooted.

"It's a pleasant room, this," said the Sergeant, "and I like his Eastern bits and pieces."

Bryce agreed. "Yes, a lot of Moorish influence in here, certainly. That's particularly typical of the style," he said, pointing to a double-width stool on short wooden legs, its padded top covered in a beautifully intricate carpet. "You can lose yourself following the designs in those little rugs, they're so complicated."

He suddenly sat forwards. "Sometimes, Sergeant, they craft those stools so they can be used as ottomans. That particular one is an example of the type that doesn't open, because it's too shallow. But given the other adaptations Allen has made…"

He was on his feet and beside the attractive piece of furniture before finishing his thought. The longer sides showed the DCS there were no hinges – something which Lomax could hardly have missed in his earlier search of the room. Undeterred, Bryce bent forwards, grasped the carpeted top and pulled very hard.

The entire stool rose up from the floor in one piece in his hands.

"I thought something shifted slightly within the stool as I manhandled it. Hold a couple of the legs down while I try again."

Between them, the detectives wrestled the top off the stool, revealing a space inside no more than three inches deep. Crammed tightly into it was everything they were searching for. At the same time they saw why the stool would never have given up its contents easily – the inner sides of the home-made lid had been liberally smeared with adhesive.

The detectives now gazed happily at not just one, but two automatic pistols, packed with the dress they were expecting, the yellow cardigan, and the blonde wig.

Bryce was triumphant. "Finally, we have success!"

He eyed the two pistols. One was indeed a Walther PPK, with a silencer already screwed onto the barrel. The other was a weapon he had heard about but had never seen before. It also had a suppressor, but this appeared to be part of the gun itself.

"Both these, plus the Colt that Allen was carrying, are of the same calibre," Bryce remarked. "But if that one," he pointed "proves to be the one which killed McLeish and Farncombe, whoever guessed in 1945 the weapon was a Walther was correct. Still could be the Colt, though. We'll leave it to Hendon to tell us.

"But this," he pointed at the gun with the integral suppressor, "is a real rarity. A Welrod Mark II. Designed for special forces in the last war. No use to Allen in the cases we've looked at, because it's bolt operated, and you can't fire a second shot without using two hands. A very, very unusual weapon."

Lomax, after the drama of the morning, felt an urge to lift his spirits. He reached down, shook out the wig and put it on.

"Suits you, Sergeant, but I don't think police regulations will allow you to wear it to work – unless you want a transfer to the vice squad, of course!"

Bryce was pleased that his hunch about Allen keeping everything close to hand was correct. When making his running assessments of how a case was progressing, he always behaved like the barrister he used to be, anticipating how opposing counsel would react. Before embarking on the raid, he had already run some grim scenarios in his head in the event that they might not discover the gun and the wig.

Had that been the outcome of their searching, the tables might have been completely turned. He could see Allen's barrister claiming that the police had been unable to present any substantial evidence to even prove his client's *involvement* in the murders he was charged with, much less his *guilt*.

Worse still, it might have been successfully argued that Allen, an Englishman in his castle and minding his own business that morning, had come under terrifying and simultaneous armed attack by multiple officers on both sides of his property, for absolutely no reason.

Moreover, that he had been badly – not to mention unlawfully – injured, in a wrongful police raid. Allen's shooting of Davey and Firth would no doubt be played as justified self-defence against a deadly force. Although that would no doubt have been countered by the Crown pointing out that a number of the 'attackers' were in uniform, and therefore obviously policemen, there would still have been things to confuse the jury and undermine confidence in the Crown's case.

These now-irrelevant legal arguments dismissed from his mind, Bryce told Lomax, "We'll carry on looking elsewhere for the rest of the evidence: the van, and Billy, if we can find him. But I'm pleased to say I believe we could secure a conviction with what we already have."

He checked his watch. Holding out Allen's keyring he said, "It's time you took a well-earned break, Lomax, after which you should try and find a home for these two extra keys.

"Ask around. Bound to be lock-up garages about. And it's always possible he rented another domestic garage. You know the sort of arrangement, someone who doesn't have a car and likes a bit of extra income. Talk to the neighbours.

I'll bet they've never seen him in that wig and dress, but they might have seen something else.

"Bag up the three pistols. The clothing and wig can stay in the stool – it'll just about fit on the back seat, I think. My first priority is to get everything booked into the evidence store at Leman Street for now. Then I'm calling in at the King George to see how Davey and Firth are, before going back to Leman Street to make decisions about Palmer, among other things."

"Will you let him go sir?"

"I may have to. I don't expect to be that long in Leman Street, so find me back at the Yard when you've finished, Sergeant."

Bryce picked up the stool and headed to his car. Lomax followed with the evidence bags containing the guns and locked these into the boot to join the fake ID cards, bullets, and cash.

CHAPTER 14

Although it wasn't visiting hours the Chief Superintendent was allowed to see his men. They were side by side in a small ward of four beds, wearing hospital pyjamas. They both greeted him cheerily enough as he positioned a chair between their beds.

"I'm extremely sorry you find yourselves here, gentlemen," he said, and explained how Allen had been looking out of a rear window. "It's some consolation that you're not as badly injured as you might have been, but I still feel wretched because it shouldn't have happened."

"Not your fault, sir," replied Davey. "I was every bit as prepared to shoot as you were, but he had the element of surprise that we thought was ours and he was a bit quicker – that's all there was to it.

"Anyway, the doc says I'll be laid up here for a few days, then hobbling about at home. After which, I can expect to be deskbound for a bit at work until everything's come together again in my leg." He managed a smile. "Probably worse places for me to be with Peggy at her sister's. The food here is bound to be better than what I could put together for myself at home."

Firth told the DCS that he had received much the same diagnosis and advice from the doctor who had examined him. The difficulty in his case was the restricted movement in his dominant right arm, leaving him to rely on a left arm which he jokingly described as being as useful to him as a second left foot.

The three officers chatted for a while, Bryce insisting on taking a note of what each man would need for his stay before leaving to find ZacharyAllen in an adjoining ward.

He was surprised to find a white-coated doctor was only just attending to the prisoner. This delay was soon explained by the medic, who said that a coach accident involving children had swallowed up all available hands soon after Davey and Field had received attention. As instructed, Sergeant Prentice was still attached to Allen, with Sergeant Brooker looming nearby.

"All right, Prentice. I think with three of us here you can take off the cuffs for a minute, and let the doctor see what needs to be done."

"Thanks. I've given him a strong sedative which has knocked him out, so he won't be doing any running for another hour or so – and before that we'll get him under general anaesthetic. He has a bullet hole in the shoulder with no exit wound, so we'll need to locate that. The shot in the arm was in and out, but it's smashed the humerus; we'll have to do something about that."

The doctor continued with his ministrations. Without looking up he asked, "From all these precautions, I gather this man is dangerous."

"Extremely. Let me put it this way: he won't be needing his arm for more than another two or three months. Just patch him up enough to face trial, please."

To the Sergeants he said. "Stay with him, gentlemen, including by the door of the operating theatre looking in. As soon as he's out of theatre, conscious or not, put the cuffs on again. I've arranged with H Division for men to come and relieve you, so you can look forward to that. Thank you both for your help today."

Bryce returned to Leman Street, where the Desk Sergeant handed him a message. Reading it as he walked to his temporary room, he saw that Mrs Pickford wanted him to call her.

He did this immediately, and learned that a solicitor had telephoned, claiming he had urgent information regarding the Griswell Road murder.

Bryce called the number his Secretary gave him, and found himself connected to a small firm in Loughton.

"Unusual situation for me, Chief Superintendent," said Mr Brackenbury, the solicitor. "Your murder victim Joseph Farncombe came to see me recently. I'd never seen him before, and it turned out he didn't even live near here. He wanted to swear out an affidavit. He'd typed it out himself and once he'd signed it and I'd witnessed it, it was sealed in an envelope, my instruction being to open it on his death from whatever cause.

"I told him he must be sure to make arrangements with his family, or another representative, to contact me in the event of his death. But he insisted it was absolutely unnecessary and couldn't be talked round on the point.

"Naturally, I asked him how I would know he'd died if someone close to him didn't contact the firm, but he wouldn't say.

"I now believe, Chief Superintendent, Mr Farncombe's insistence that no one would need to inform me indicates that he foresaw his death would be a newsworthy one. Which is why I'm contacting you about his affidavit, because from my point of view the nature of his death rather reinforces everything in it."

"You've read it?" queried Bryce.

"I have. And even though it's not in the best King's English, the gist is very plain. He confessed that he fenced stolen goods and recorded details of quite a number of transactions, all allegedly at the indirect behest of a man named Samuel Palmer, who sent his agents along with the goods.

"Incidentally, he included two addresses where he stored the goods, and where to find the keys for access, which I'm sure will be of interest to you. Mr Farncombe also stated that if he died violently, his death will have been brought about on the orders of this Samuel Palmer.

"I have no idea how much of what he's put is true, but I think I owe it to my late client to support him even in death. On my reading of the affidavit, I don't think there is evidence for a charge of murder, but I think there's ample to allow you to arrest Samuel Palmer on suspicion of various burglary offences, assuming you can find him."

"Thank you, Mr Brackenbury. As it happens we have Palmer under lock and key at present, and this will help us hold onto him for longer.

"Are you in a position to give me a quick rundown of what's in the affidavit, please?"

The Solicitor was happy to read the entire document. It took him nearly ten minutes, and Bryce's smile widened as he listened.

"Thank you, you've been most helpful. Hearing all of that, I suspect Farncombe came to you precisely because you were well removed from his patch – very unlikely that anyone would see him entering your office and drawing the right conclusions. I expect you want to hang on to the original, but can you let me have a transcript, or a duplicate?"

It was agreed that a notarised copy would be prepared and sent by special messenger to Superintendent Livermore that afternoon.

Bryce returned to the front desk and asked for Palmer to be taken to an interview room, and for the custody officer to wait with him.

When the burglar was brought in, he greeted the DCS breezily, obviously expecting that his 'assistance' the day before would now result in his release. Bryce confirmed his expectations on the point, telling him that no charges relating to Farncombe's murder would be preferred at present.

Palmer's excess flesh wobbled as he chuckled in his elation. "Well ain't that dandy Mr Bryce! You an' me parting on good terms again, just like the last time when you wrongly thought you'd nabbed me."

It was the Chief Superintendent's turn to airily deliver a dose of reality. "Not really, Sam. I'm charging you with being an accessory, both before and after the fact, to various matters of burglary that Joe Farncombe identified in an affidavit.

"I also charge you with conspiracy to commit burglary, on evidence from the same source. We'll sort out the details later. No doubt you'll want a solicitor now."

Palmer, flabbergasted, said nothing, his mouth hanging open.

"Back to the cells with him, Constable."

Bryce returned to the front desk and completed the paperwork.

"Is Mr Livermore in the station, Sergeant?"

"Yes, sir."

"Call him would you, and see if he could spare me a few minutes now."

Bryce had barely sat down when the Superintendent arrived. "Good news," announced the DCS. "We now have strong evidence to charge Zachary Allen with both murders, and I hope further charges will follow."

He went on to explain about Andrew Morton-Hugh and Robert Rennie in Glasgow and their connection to the Rabid Dog case, and about those still in custody at Scotland Yard. The two men had a lengthy discussion about procedural matters.

"One other thing. Sam Palmer is in your cells here. Privately, I'm sure he ordered the hit on Farncombe, but although we're still seeking further evidence, I doubt if I can ever prove it.

"However, fresh evidence has come to light regarding his more usual activities." He briefed the Superintendent on the information from Farncombe's solicitor. "A notarised copy of the affidavit will arrive here shortly, addressed for your attention."

Livermore beamed. "Palmer's been a king-sized thorn in the rump of the police here for years. It'll be good to get him inside for a long stretch. Thank you for all you've done, sir. Much appreciated."

Bryce made two more calls before returning to Scotland Yard. The first was to the local hospital, where he was able to speak to Nurse Donaldson. He assured her that Allen was now safely in custody, but suggested that it would still be better not to share her experience.

Superintendent Fraser wasn't in to take his next call, but the DI who answered clearly knew all about the case. He promised to pass the information to his boss as soon as he returned, guaranteeing, much to Bryce's amusement, that "The Super will be skirling on his bagpipes to celebrate, and I may even do a Highland fling mysen!"

The Chief Superintendent's briefcase was packed and he was ready to leave Leman Street, but he found his gaze irresistibly drawn to the carton with the Rabid Dog murder papers, still sitting on the floor of the absent DI's office. Arrangements would be made for both boxes to be transferred to Scotland Yard in due course. In the meantime, having just spoken to George Fraser's DI, his curiosity on a certain point had been freshly piqued, and he decided he wouldn't wait for that to happen.

He took out the files with the witness statements and re-read them all. By the time he had finished, he had removed the two of interest to him, made a mental note of an address, and returned everything else to the box.

With a friendly 'until we meet again' wave for Sergeant Sawyer, the DCS left Leman Street and drove back to the Yard.

He was dictating a letter to his Secretary when Lomax arrived to speak to him. The Sergeant was almost bubbling with excitement.

"Found a lock-up, sir, and quite close by. Which makes sense I suppose, because if Allen needed to make a run for it, like he tried today, he'd want his escape vehicle to hand. Key for the padlock is the one on his key ring, as is the ignition key for the van inside. An old Singer Bantam 9, just like Vincent said, dark green. Must still be dozens like it around London. I got a nice selection of clear prints. Locked it all up, fixed for a uniformed officer to guard it until we can recover everything, and came away."

Bryce was nodding happily. "More good work, Sergeant!"

Lomax hadn't finished. "I got an address from the GPO for that Goodmayes 'phone number Nathan Scott gave us, as well. Belongs to a Billy Watt. Lives not far from Allen, but not in such a nice area. He might have a flat, but I'm guessing more likely a rented room. Small-scale crook, sir; various minor matters on record over a twenty-year period. All for dishonesty of one sort or another."

The DCS felt that in other circumstances he would have started bubbling along with Lomax at this news. Unfortunately, the fact that two of his men were in hospital was taking the shine off the way things were falling into place.

To the Sergeant he said, "Round him up on suspicion of aiding and abetting a murder and bring him in here. Take a DC if you can divert one; otherwise press-gang a PC.

"Lean on Watt hard while you're still at his place. Tell him if he has any evidence he'd better produce it sharpish. Take a quick look around anyway. While you're doing that, I'll see about the two we already have incarcerated here."

Bryce went back downstairs and instructed the Desk Sergeant to have the elderly publican brought to an interview room. A few minutes later, a worried-looking Scott arrived, the DCS telling the escorting officer to wait.

"All right, Nathan, I'm going to release you without charge. You should consider yourself very lucky indeed that we've found some bigger fish to fry. But don't get complacent and think I won't reel you in again if I hear you're involved in anything else."

Scott started to express his thanks, but Bryce interrupted him. "You can thank me for keeping you out of prison, certainly, but you may soon be homeless and jobless.

"When this business reaches court – if not before – the Licensing Justices will hear about your activities. I shouldn't be at all surprised if they decide that you're no longer a 'fit and proper person' to hold a licence.

"Book him out, Sergeant, and then find Trevor Walsh for me. And make sure you keep him cuffed."

Within ten minutes, Walsh arrived. Overnight in the cells had given him plenty of time to realise he was in deep trouble, and to visualise the consequences.

"You'll be pleased to hear that we have Zachary Allen in custody," Bryce told him. "Two bullets in him, but he'll live to meet the hangman.

"I'm going to charge you, Walsh. It may be that you'll be given a deal in return for testifying against Allen and Robert Rennie, but in my opinion you don't deserve it. Whatever happens, the streets of London will be a lot cleaner for many years when you and the likes of Sam Palmer are removed."

Bryce stood up and carried out the formalities. "You'll appear in court in the morning, and you'll want your solicitor again today, no doubt."

Walsh nodded without speaking, and Bryce signalled to the officer to take him back to the cells. He went to the front desk to sort the paperwork for the newly-charged man himself.

The Custody Sergeant mentioned that half the country's Press representatives were milling around the building. Bryce looked puzzled, seeing no sign of anyone.

"Oh, Mr Nunn told us to herd them into the training room, sir. We couldn't have them all in the foyer."

Bryce was on his way back to his office when he was intercepted by Jack Nunn.

"Reporters have been arriving thick and fast, sir. I've put them in the training room, and if it wasn't starting to rain I'd have corralled them in the car park. They're getting impatient. Do you want me to talk to them?"

"I'll do it, Jack. It'd take more time to give you a full briefing than it will for me to tell them direct. Leave it with me."

Altering his course, Bryce made for the training room. The door was open and he could hear a hubbub of noise while still in the corridor some distance away. It was not a particularly large room and was completely crammed. Some reporters were sitting at the tables and chairs, while others were obliged to stand. He decided to stay where he was in the doorway, his quick exit guaranteed when the time came to wind the meeting up.

The noise had increased as he reached the door, but now fell away almost to silence as a ripple of understanding hush descended, every reporter appreciating there could be no questions until there was quiet.

Bryce looked around, recognising a number of those present, noting that not a single paper was represented by a female.

"Gentlemen, for those who don't know me, I am Detective Chief Superintendent Bryce. I'll give you a statement, and then I'll consider answering a few questions."

He gave the reporters a fair summary of everything that had happened, culminating with a bare outline of the shoot-out earlier in the day.

"Apart from the man we have in custody

following the raid this morning, there are three more men in custody on matters directly related to murder. Two are in Glasgow, and one here in London. Enquiries are continuing, and I anticipate that more charges will be laid.

"That's my statement, gentlemen. Ask whatever you wish, but I don't guarantee to answer."

The hubbub immediately resumed, with questions being shouted from all around the room. Bryce shook his head, and held up his hand for silence.

"Hopeless," he said. "I don't doubt that most of your questions will be the same. Let's try this another way. He looked around the room.

"Jeremy, you were first on the scene, so the first question is yours to ask."

"What's the name of the gunman, which police officers got shot, what are their injuries, what are the gunman's injuries, and who fired the shots which took him out?"

"Five questions, but I suppose everyone in the room wants the answers to all of them. I'm not releasing the names of the police officers yet. Although neither is badly hurt, in one case it hasn't been possible to notify the next of kin yet, and it's hardly fair if a wife learns from the newspapers that her husband has been shot.

"I will tell you that one was a uniformed officer, and the other a detective. One officer received a bullet in the arm, and the other in the leg. In each case the bullet passed through without serious damage – flesh wounds, in other words. Both men will be discharged from hospital sooner rather than later.

"Nor am I releasing the name of the arrested man. I'll give you that after he is charged.

"The gunman was shot twice, by me, in the shoulder and arm. His injuries are worse than my officers', but even so he won't be kept in hospital for long. When he's discharged he'll appear before a magistrate and then be transferred to Pentonville to await trial."

Several reporters called out further questions, and even more hands were raised.

"Let it not be said that I favour journalists I know," said Bryce. He pointed to a reporter he didn't recall seeing before. "You young man – who are you, which paper do you represent, and what is your question?"

The lad, who couldn't have been more than twenty, blushed and stood up. "Max Adair, from the East and West Ham Gazette. Could you tell us which hospital the injured suspect is in?"

The DCS couldn't help but join in the laughter that met this question from Adair's more experienced colleagues.

"Sorry, Max, no. You can't go and interview him, for obvious reasons. If I divulge where he is, the only result will be that the hospital is disrupted by a lot of reporters asking questions which the staff either can't or won't want to answer."

He pointed to another man. "You next."

This reporter was a grizzled chap in his sixties. The DCS thought that he must have been around for a good number of years but hadn't seen him before.

"Lester Bingham, Romford and Havering News. My question is this. You imply that the arrested man is responsible for both murders, but the three others you have in custody – which murder are they involved with?"

"All three, including the two in Glasgow are, or shortly will be, charged in connection with the Rabid Dog killing of Gordon McLeish.

"We do have another person in custody, arrested on suspicion of involvement with this week's murder. That investigation is ongoing, and at present he has only been charged with unrelated matters."

Bryce looked around the room and selected another reporter he knew. "All right Declan, you take a turn."

"In the Dog case, it was always stated and never contradicted that the killer was a woman. Witnesses reported that Monday's was a woman too. You've used the term 'man' several times this morning, Philip. When did you learn that it wasn't a woman – or are you saying that the person you've arrested didn't actually carry out the murders himself, and there's some female killer still out there."

Bryce hesitated. "We learned the killer was a man on Monday morning, and discovered his identity at the same time. You can all assure your readers that we are not looking for any female in connection with this matter."

"A supplementary, then, Philip. You're saying this was a bloke in drag, both times?"

"I'm saying that on both occasions the police are satisfied that the killer was a man wearing female clothing and accoutrements, yes.

"One last question, gentlemen." He pointed to an earnest-looking young man.

"Reggie Bryson from the News of the World – and it's probably obvious to you and many of the others here that I'm only standing in for our crime team today! I understand that the real identity of the Rabid Dog victim was never discovered, but you've given us a name today. When did you uncover it, and were both victims men of good character?"

Bryce laughed. "Your colleagues would be proud, Reggie – those are very good questions, which I think I can answer.

"Some of you are old enough to recall that the first victim was carrying false identity papers. We only discovered his real name this week. All I'll say in answer to your second question is that both victims were known to, and had records with, one police force or another.

"I emphasise, though, that their murders are in no way excusable, and that the police will pursue their murders just as expeditiously as we would pursue the killer of some popular paragon. And indeed, I hope you can see that's what we have been doing.

"Now, gentlemen, enough. Disperse, please."

A fresh hullabaloo broke out, but Bryce ignored it, slipping out of the door, where he found his deputy leaning against the wall, smiling.

"Glad you did that and not me, sir," said Nunn as he and the DCS returned to their floor. "Like a pack of wolves, they are. Here's hoping that will satisfy them until tomorrow."

"Probably not even that long. The Yard really needs some sort of Press Bureau to handle this sort of thing. I can't have you tied up with it, either. Find someone to field all the Press calls. A civilian helper if we have someone suitable who can think on his or her feet, and who can be briefed on what to say and what not to say."

Back at his office, Bryce found Mrs Pickford hovering. "Sergeant Lomax rang, sir, and asks if you'll call him back at Leman Street."

The DCS picked up his telephone. He was swiftly connected to the Whitechapel police station. The officer answering advised that DS Lomax was standing beside him, before handing over the receiver.

"Hello sir. I've gone against your orders and brought Billy Watt into Leman Street. Reason is, something he told me makes me think that when you hear it you'll want to come here and talk to

Palmer again. So I thought rather than take Watt to the Yard I'd lock him up here instead. If that's wrong, I'll bring him to you now."

"Don't tell me he's prepared to finger Palmer?"

"In a nutshell, yes, sir. And others."

"Oh frabjous day! You've made the right decision, Sergeant, well done. I'll join you in an hour or less. Whoever you took with you, thank him and send him back to normal duties."

Bryce decided to make his second journey to Whitechapel that day by tube, calculating that he could get a lift back with Lomax.

With a brief apology to Mrs Pickford, who was hoping to get him to sign papers, he walked to Westminster underground station and only had to wait a few minutes for an eastbound train.

Forty minutes later he was back in Leman Street police station, where he found Lomax, a metal box under his arm, chatting to the Desk Sergeant. Both officers looked extremely happy as they greeted the DCS.

"I take it I can still have DI Carr's room?"

"All yours, sir," confirmed Sawyer.

Putting an old chocolate tin down on the desk, Lomax began sharing his news before he had taken his seat. "We picked Watt up, no trouble; downtrodden sort of a chap. I told him he was under arrest and then said what you told me. 'Sit down, I've got something to say to you,' he said. I told him I needed to caution him, and did so, but he waved it aside and started talking.

"He obviously knew what case we were on and asked straight out if we'd arrested anyone else. I said we had someone for both the Rabid Dog and the Griswell Road murders. He laughed; he was almost hysterical. 'Oh dearie me; he's done several more than that'.

"When he'd calmed down a bit, he had a lot more to say." Lomax read from his notes. "'The bugger's 'ad an 'old over me for years; something I done in my youth. He don't blackmail me for money. Just makes it clear that if I don't do these jobs for him, he'll drop me in it. I can tell you who he's done in from the Dog killing onwards. And I can tell you who ordered each one.'

"That's when he got up and went to a drawer. We were on him in a flash, thinking he was going to pull a gun on us. All he pulled out was this old chocolate tin, saying, 'Gold dust for you; a noose for Allen and a few more alongside him.'

"Couldn't believe my eyes when he opened the tin, sir, as you'll see for yourself. He's kept all the envelopes addressed to 'Mrs A' and he's kept all the notes inside them."

Bryce was also disbelieving. "Utter madness on his part. Suicidal really, if Allen had realised. But you won't hear me grumbling, Sergeant!"

"There are eight notes, sir. All have a telephone number. A couple also have writing – 'very urgent indeed', or 'within a month'. There's also a little book with twelve names and numbers.

"The eight notes have only three different telephone numbers between them – all of which appear in the book against a name. Four have the number for Walsh, two are Palmer's number, and two are someone called Parkinson. Watt says Parkinson is dead.

"We opened the notes with hankies, in case we can lift prints off them."

Bryce approved of this, and had already decided that he would not disturb the contents of the tin any further himself.

Lomax was continuing, his enthusiasm mounting. "And there's even more! Billy confirmed the arrangement with Nathan Scott was that he would telephone Billy as soon as a message arrived in the pub. Billy sent a lad to collect it and immediately rang the enclosed number. He'd be given the name, and sometimes more details, like a location. After that, he contacted Allen, and passed all the information on.

"Now he knows we've got Allen, Walsh and Palmer safely inside, Watt seems quite keen to testify."

Bryce's smile had got progressively wider as the Sergeant made his report.

"Has he requested a solicitor?"

"No, sir."

"Good. Very good. Let's see if we can get a formal statement."

A little over an hour later, Bryce had the statement he wanted, Watt being very keen to co-operate.

"That bastard Zak used me for years, an' made a mint. The others, too. I 'ardly ever met 'im in the last four or so years – only a couple of times. But once I was with 'im and 'e's on the dog'n'bone to Sam. 'Oh, Billy's quite safe,' he says.

"So Sam starts givin' me little jobs to do – always the risky ones wot 'e 'needs to steer clear of. Never paid a fair whack neither.

"I'm sick of it all an' sick of the lot of 'em. I made one lousy mistake when I wasn't much more'n a kid and it's trapped me for the rest of me life. Now I want out of it all – any which way I can."

The detectives were struck by the fact that Billy Watt thought prison would be preferable to his current existence. There was something particularly pathetic in his regret, and both wondered what the nature of his 'one lousy mistake' had been.

With his statement signed, Bryce asked Watt if he wanted to see a solicitor. This was declined.

"I aint got one. Never saw no point in 'em."

The DCS shook his head. "You've never faced this level of charge before, Billy. Tomorrow, if you appear in court without a solicitor, I think the beak will see if you can get a dock brief. You really do need someone. Anyway, I'm charging you with aiding and abetting Zachary Allen in various murders. That's not a capital offence, but it's still very serious.

"Take him back, please Sergeant, and get them to bring Sam Palmer up. And don't let them see each other – we don't want another murder!"

Billy Watt scowled as he heard that Palmer was in the building. For a moment, it looked as though he was going to spit on the floor in disgust, before withdrawing quietly.

A few minutes later, Palmer was brought in.

Bryce made a show of studying Billy Watt's statement on the table in front of him, and didn't so much as glance in Palmer's direction. "Don't bother to sit down, Sam. I now have more evidence to use against you. I'm charging you with being an accessory before the fact in the murder of Joseph Farncombe. Take him away again."

Palmer was so surprised that he said nothing as Lomax took him by the arm and started leading him out of the interview room. At the door he suddenly turned and said "I suppose Zak is squealing like a stuck pig. He always was a coward."

When the Sergeant came back, he found his boss still sitting, looking pensive.

"That last remark was also evidence, wasn't it sir?"

"Yes indeed. Make a note in your pocketbook. I'm just musing about all this. If Palmer hadn't decided to put a contract on Farncombe, we'd probably never have solved the old pub case. And now, it looks as though this may solve few other murder cases, and we'll certainly hand the information about those to whichever police forces are appropriate."

"The one from Leeds where Hendon is checking the bullets, sir; that one's definitely on Billy's list. One of Walsh's."

"Looks like we've got another three cases then, five if we can include the ones from the deceased Parkinson.

"In other circumstances, I'd be saying we'll go straight back to the Yard when we're done here. But I've been mentally chasing something that hasn't made sense to me with the Rabid Dog case, and since I'm back here again I may as well see if I can settle the matter once and for all, with your help, Sergeant."

Seeing Lomax's quizzical expression, he said, "take another break, while I quickly brief Mr Livermore about the latest on Sam Palmer, and deal with the paperwork for his new charge.

"Then we're going to pay Mr Eric Mannington a visit, and I'll explain what's been bothering me on the way."

CHAPTER 15

Bryce had also given himself time to grab some refreshment before he and Lomax drove to the lodging house. Prior enquiries at Leman Street had confirmed that Mannington still ran the premises, and that there had been visits by officers from that station to speak to both residents and the owner.

Before driving the unmarked Wolseley to Mannington's address, Bryce pulled out the pub barmaid's witness statement, and the lodging house keeper's.

"Take a look at those, Sergeant, as we go along, and tell me if anything strikes you."

Lomax hadn't seen either of the statements before and read them carefully. Reluctantly, and disappointed with himself, he admitted nothing at all jumped out at him as odd. "They both seem straightforward to me, sir. Although you can see the barmaid's is much less informative, on face value."

"I agree. But now reconsider the statements with what we've learned – having never met him ourselves – about McLeish's origins."

Lomax, still puzzled, carefully read the statements for a second time. Understanding dawned.

"McLeish was from the Gorbals. He would have had a strong Glaswegian accent, but there's no mention of an accent in Mannington's statement. Yet he hasn't hidden that they made arrangements between themselves – implying conversation."

"Exactly."

Lomax continued. "The barmaid mentions, almost in passing when she describes her interactions with McLeish, that he never spoke to her. But Mannington, who lives in the same house and with far more opportunity, is silent on the point. You'd think they must have spoken sometimes, wouldn't you?"

"I would. Let's see how Eric explains withholding a piece of information which, in theory, would have turned that old investigation in a different – and perhaps much more successful – direction."

The detectives found 44 Plether Road. Bryce parked the car a little way up the street and they were soon knocking on the door.

Mannington himself answered, mop in hand, and a bucket at his feet. He had obviously been actively engaged in cleaning. His shirtsleeves were rolled up, revealing an anchor tattooed on one forearm. Small splashes of water were noticeable on the shins of his trousers. He gave a disdainful look when Lomax showed his warrant card.

"Never ends with you lot, does it? I'm surprised you don't take a room here yourselves. Then you could spy on me and disrupt my day whenever you feel like it. Save me the bother of opening the door."

Bryce turned to Lomax. "First rate idea, actually, and always heartwarming when citizens are so helpful. Make a note of the offer, Sergeant."

This was an unexpected rejoinder to his own sarcasm, and Mannington wasn't pleased to hear it. He angrily dumped his mop into the bucket. Arms akimbo, he demanded, "What d'you want now, eh?"

"We want to know why you didn't tell investigators six years ago that your lodger, the one who was murdered in the Rabid Dog and whom we know now was Gordon McLeish, spoke with a Scottish accent.

Mannington's retort was immediate. "No he never! How could he?"

Lomax answered. "How could he? Very easily! He came from the Gorbals district of Glasgow."

"So what if he did. He could have come from Timbuctoo and still not spoken with an accent."

"Are you saying that when he spoke to you, he sounded English not Scottish?" asked Lomax.

The lodging house keeper snorted, but didn't deign to give the Sergeant an explanation.

Bryce shook his head. "No. I think what Mr Mannington is telling us – or rather not telling us – is that McLeish didn't have any accent at all. As with the barmaid, he's telling us he never spoke."

Lomax was non-plussed by this. He said no more and let his Chief unscramble the mystery.

Mannington gave a slow handclap. "Everything was in writing. Beginning with the information that he'd had cancer of the tongue and couldn't speak any more, cos they'd had to chop it all out."

Bryce guffawed. "He opened his mouth nice and wide and said 'ahhh' to prove it to you, did he?"

Mannington also laughed, now far more relaxed and sensing he had the upper hand. "No need for that 'cos it didn't matter to me either way, did it? Nothing illegal in me fixing a nice fat rate for the room and agreeing the terms. All of which went in my statement." He checked himself. "Well, not the rate for the room. That's always confidential business between me and my gentlemen."

Bryce nodded. He could not contradict the claim because it was indeed all in the statement. It was also true that had the investigators been told today's revelation, it would have taken them no further forward.

The DCS and Lomax left Mannington to his mopping and returned to their car.

"Well, that almost settles that," said Bryce as he made a three point turn in the road and started the journey back to the Yard. "It still leaves a lot of unanswered questions, but I suspect we'll never get to the bottom of them, and will just have to accept that sometimes we don't get to know everything."

"Where do you think all of McLeish's money is, sir? Allen must have had thousands on him in those three rolls I took out of his pockets. But McLeish apparently had nothing, even though you said Mr Fraser reported that he'd got away with maybe five grand."

"Yes, intriguing isn't it? As counter-intuitive as it may seem, he may have banked it somewhere, perhaps even using his real name and ID. More likely though, using the false name and fake ID. We could try to find the account, but since there may not even be one I don't propose to waste any time looking. If he did open an account, with no one making a claim any money will eventually simply be absorbed by the bank into their profits."

"How about he stashed it in his room and Mannington found it?"

"Definitely possible, but unlikely, I think. It was six years ago, and I find it hard to believe that he'd still be mopping floors and changing bedlinen at 44 Plether Road if he'd laid hands on big money."

Bryce didn't share his last thought. That maybe it was Sergeant Blakely who had found the money. The policeman seemed to have unexpectedly come into money from an unknown source, and retired early to live in South America.

The DCS knew from the investigation reports that it was Blakely who had first spoken to Mannington in his house-to-house enquiries. With the Leman Street CID undermanned after the war, it was Blakely who had carried out the searching and the fingerprinting alone.

He drove on, turning over the various options in his mind. As much as he didn't want to suspect 'one of his own', he felt Blakely's destination – there was no extradition treaty between Britain and Brazil – left an unfortunately unpleasant taste.

Lomax broke into his thoughts, and took them in a different direction.

"I reckon congratulations are in order, sir; it's another win for C4 isn't it?"

"Yes, but we had a huge amount of luck. If Farncombe had died without speaking – as Allen no doubt assumed he had – we'd never have got anywhere. We wouldn't have had the name and wouldn't have even known the killer was male.

"Also, you personally had luck in just happening to meet young Vincent – and you need that sort of luck in our job.

"We were also very fortunate that Allen didn't kill our two officers. You heard me tell everyone to shoot to kill if he drew a gun. I should have acted on my own order and fired a full second sooner than I did. I blame myself for what happened, and that will go in my report.

"So no, I'm not taking any pride in this case.

"You, on the other hand, have done very well indeed from start to finish, and I shall say so in my report. It's a few years away yet, but you'll certainly make DI sooner rather than later."

Lomax didn't say it out loud, but he thought his boss was being characteristically modest. Instead, quietly happy, he wondered if he could find some grapes to take to his wounded colleagues for evening visiting hour.

****

ACCESORIES AND ABETTORS ACT 1861

Section 1
Accessories before the Fact may be tried and punished as Principals.

Whosoever shall become an Accessory before the Fact to any Felony, whether the same be a Felony at Common Law or by virtue of any Act passed or to be passed, may be indicted, tried, convicted, and punished in all respects as if he were a principal Felon.

Section 2
Accessories before the Fact may be indicted as such, or as substantive Felons.

Whosoever shall counsel, procure, or **command any other Person to commit any Felony,** whether the same be a Felony at Common Law or by virtue of any Act passed or to be passed, **shall be guilty of Felony, and may be indicted and convicted either as an Accessory before the Fact to the principal Felony**, together with the principal Felon, or after the Conviction of the principal Felon, **or may be indicted and convicted of a substantive Felony** whether the principal Felon shall or shall not have been previously convicted, or shall or shall not be amenable to Justice, and may thereupon be punished in the same Manner as any Accessory before the Fact to the same Felony, if convicted as an Accessory, may be punished.

THE PHILIP BRYCE SERIES

A series of detective stories featuring London police detective Philip Bryce in the 1940s and 1950s.

The Bedroom Window Murder

The Courthouse Murder

The Felixstowe Murder

Multiples Of Murder

Death At Mistram Manor

Machinations Of A Murderer

Suspicions Of A Parlourmaid And The Norfolk Railway Murders

This Village Is Cursed

The Amateur Detective

Demands With Menaces

Murder In Academe

The King's Bench Walk Murder And Death In The Boardroom

To be published shortly

The Devon Murders

To be published shortly

Other books by this author are shown on the following page.

BOOKS BY THIS AUTHOR

Death Of A Safebreaker

1937. A burglar is found shot dead in the home of Viscount Tallis, a wealthy industrialist. The man was equipped with a stethoscope, and appears to have been attempting to open a safe in the study. Tallis himself is in the middle of the Atlantic Ocean, on his way to America on Government business. Although various members of his family are present in the house, together with guests, nobody has access to the safe – nobody even knows what it might contain. It isn't even clear if the safebreaker succeeded in opening it.

Detective Inspector Tommy Rees is given the case. Rees is approaching retirement, and has never had to investigate a murder in his rural county before. Initially he has little choice about taking advice from two or three people who are themselves on the suspect list.

Eventually, he must rely on the goodwill – and

deep pockets – of the absent Lord Tallis.

Death Of A Juror

1936. In Lincoln, two men are on trial on charges of manslaughter. The trial has hardly started when one of the jurors dies. It is quickly found that she has been poisoned.

Chief Inspector Acton, already present in the courthouse for other reasons, takes charge of the investigations. A suspect soon emerges – and anonymous letters point the detectives towards the same man.

But is all as it seems? And even if the suspect is innocent of this murder, are his hands quite clean?

DCI Acton and his colleagues filter out the red herrings, and arrive at a solution.

The Failed Lawyer

A story set in 1952 London

At school, Morris Major almost obsessively read every crime fiction novel he could get his hands on, and from about the age of twelve decided that he wanted to be a detective of some sort. However, he found later that there were considerable difficulties even to start on this career path, and by the time he left school he had reluctantly abandoned that ambition, and decided to be a barrister instead.

In due course he was called to the bar, but then had to start his National Service. That duty completed, he returned to the barristers' chambers where he had undergone his pupillage, and prepared to start work.

Unfortunately, things did not go well. Morris had certain idiosyncrasies which were incompatible with the requirements to advise clients and to address courts. After a number of embarrassing incidents, he resigned from his chambers.

However, after that nadir, things began to look up – first of all in his hitherto largely barren love life.

But by a complete accident of fate, he became involved in a sudden death. Using his innate intelligence, he was was able to persuade the police that their solution – although self-evidently the correct one – was in fact wrong.

To be a private detective was, of course, one of the options he had dreamed about as a schoolboy, but having been thrust into a situation where he had been inadvertently cast into such a role, he found the reality not entirely to his liking. Yes, it was satisfying to work out what had really happened, but this pleasure had to be balanced against a great deal of unpleasantness.

The experience did, however, give him an idea.

Two subsequent incidents concerning the police sufficed to convince him that being a detective – whether a policeman or one of the the private variety so beloved by crime fiction authors and their readers – was a profession that he was glad he had been unable to enter.

He determined to start a totally different career.